SCARY
MYSTERIES
FOR SLEEP-OVERS

By Allen B. Ury
Illustrated by Mia Tavonatti

An RGA Book

PRICE STERN SLOAN
Los Angeles

Copyright © 1996 RGA Publishing Group, Inc.
Published by Price Stern Sloan, Inc.,
A member of The Putnam & Grosset Group, New York, New York.

ISBN: 0-8431-8220-2
First Edition
1 3 5 7 9 10 8 6 4 2

Library of Congress Cataloging-in-Publication Data

Ury, Allen B.
    Scary mysteries for sleep-overs/by Allen B. Ury; illustrated by Mia Tavonatti.
        p. cm.
    "An RGA book."
    "#1"
    Summary: Presents ten stories with frightening twists, including "Deadman's Curve," "Suspended Animation," and "Public Enemy."
    ISBN 0-8431-8220-2
    1. Horror tales, American. 2. Children stories, American.
[1. Horror stories. 2. Short stories.] I. Tavoniatti, Mia, ill.
II. Title
PZ7.U694Sc 1996   95-49290
                                                                  CIP
                                                                   AC

Designed by Cheryl Carrington

contents

To my high school chemistry teacher,
who told me to stick to writing.

—A. B. U.

To my niece, Alexa.

—M. T.

the doppelganger

oach Greeley cleared his throat. "And this season's Most Valuable Player Award goes to—Russell McShane!" he announced proudly. Instantly thunderous applause swept through Truman Junior High School's cafeteria where the twenty members of the championship soccer team and their families had gathered for the annual end-of-the-season awards dinner.

Russell, a tall, handsome eighth grader with shoulder-length blond hair and a winning smile, bounded up the center aisle, turned to wave to the audience, then shook Coach Greeley's large, leathery hand and accepted his award.

As the applause died down, the coach leaned into the microphone to speak. "For the record, Russell here scored a total of twenty-two points this season," he announced. "That's an average of two-point-two goals per game—the highest in the district." He paused and scanned the crowd. "I'd like to add that he accomplished this amazing feat while still maintaining a 3.6 grade-point average, proving that it's possible to have both brains and brawn."

Another round of enthusiastic applause filled the cafeteria.

"Personally I'd like to thank you, Russell, for making this our best season yet," the coach continued, now looking Russell straight in the eye. "You're a true leader, and a great team player. You're one of a kind, and it's been an honor to be your coach."

"Thank you, Coach Greeley," Russell responded with a smile as once again he shook the man's strong, firm hand. "I couldn't have done it without you . . . or the team. The award really belongs to everyone."

With that Russell and Coach Greeley stood side by side, while several photographers from the school and local newspapers, as well as parents snapped flash photos of the pair. More applause, accompanied by hoots and whistles from Russell's teammates, provided the appropriate festive background.

But at the back of the room, hidden in the shadows, some-one was watching the ceremony with cold, scornful eyes. This boy was unmoved by the honors being bestowed upon Russell McShane. In fact, he felt only hate and loathing for the love and appreciation being showered upon the soccer star. His heart filled with envy. This angry boy wanted revenge, and one way or another, he knew he would have it.

■ ■ ■ ■

The following Monday afternoon, after the bell rang ending his math class, Russell was just stepping into the crowded hallway when he saw Mr. Kelso, his heavyset science teacher, waving him over. The man looked troubled.

"Russell, I need to speak with you for a moment," Mr. Kelso said, ushering him toward a private corner.

"Sure, Mr. Kelso," Russell said casually. "What's up?"

"We have a bit of a problem," the science teacher replied, keeping his voice low. "One of our new stereo microscopes is missing. It's a five-hundred-dollar instrument that won't be easy to replace. Anything you can do to help see that it gets returned would be greatly appreciated."

"No problem, Mr. Kelso," Russell said with a shrug. He wondered why he'd been singled out for this unusual assignment. "If I hear anything about it, I'll let you know."

He turned to leave, but Mr. Kelso grabbed his arm and held him back.

"I'm serious about this, Russell," the science teacher said, his voice now taking on a threatening tone. "I really want that microscope back."

"Sure, I understand," Russell replied nervously. "But why are you asking me? I mean, I don't exactly hang out with the kind of kids who steal school property."

"I was hoping it wouldn't have to come to this, Russell, but you leave me no choice," Mr. Kelso said sternly. And with that he reached into his jacket and pulled out a pocket-sized, spiral-bound notebook. "Does this look familiar?"

"My assignment notebook!" Russell exclaimed, breaking out in a smile. "I thought I'd lost it. Where did you find it?"

He reached for the notebook, but Mr. Kelso held it out of the boy's reach.

"I found it this morning next to the cabinet the microscope was taken from," Mr. Kelso reported, his expression grim. "Would you care to explain that?"

"Wait a minute," Russell said, his heart suddenly racing as if he'd just finished a hundred-yard sprint. "You think *I* stole your microscope? But that's crazy! Why would I do something like that?"

"Are you telling me you had nothing to do with the theft?" Mr. Kelso asked.

"I'm absolutely, positively sure," Russell stated firmly. "I had nothing to do with it."

"All right, Russell, I believe you," said Mr. Kelso, returning the spiral-bound notebook. "You've always been one of my best students, and I believe you are an honorable young man. I'm sorry that this happened."

"So am I," Russell said, nervously slipping the notebook into his backpack. "And if I do find out anything about that microscope, I'll let you know right away."

"Thank you, Russell, I appreciate it," the science teacher said, giving Russell a reassuring pat on the back.

But even as Russell headed down the hall toward his next class, he could still feel Mr. Kelso's eyes staring at him, as if the man didn't trust him. Russell thought hard. How *had* his notebook gotten into the science lab? He knew he hadn't been anywhere near that room since the previous Friday, yet the notebook itself contained the assignments he'd jotted in it the following Monday.

There was only one explanation: Someone had stolen the notebook from his backpack and had used it to try to frame him. But who'd do something like that? And why? It was a mystery Russell was determined to solve.

He began by retracing his steps on the previous Friday as best he could remember them. After entering the school he'd gone to his locker, then to his homeroom class. Next he'd had math, and after that, English. At 12:30 he'd gone to the cafeteria for lunch. During this entire morning his backpack had never been out of his sight. Except . . .

"The cafeteria!" he exclaimed. Russell now remembered leaving his backpack at a table while he'd gone across the room

8

to talk with Blake, another member of the soccer team. He'd only been gone for a minute or two, but it was possible that the notebook could have been taken during that time.

"Hey George, did you see anyone go into my backpack while I was talking with Blake at lunch last Friday?" he later asked his friend who had eaten with him that day.

George replied with a shrug, "No one but you."

For a second Russell was confused. "What do you mean, no one but me?" he finally asked. "I didn't open my backpack. I know because I only had my books and pens in there—not my lunch. That day I bought my lunch with money I took from my back pocket." Russell became agitated. "So you see, I had no reason to open my backpack, right?"

"All right, all right!" George said, putting his hands up defensively. "What are you getting so upset about?" He paused for a moment as if trying to remember something. "Wait a minute. I did see you taking something out of your backpack. I remember you left the table for a minute, then you came back and took your notebook out of it. I remember because I asked you where you'd gotten that cool T-shirt, since you weren't wearing it when you left. But you didn't say anything, and just took off."

"*T-shirt*?" Russell inquired, his patience growing thin. "I wasn't wearing a T-shirt yesterday."

"It was black and had a Flying Diamonds logo on the front," George explained, referring to a popular rock band. "That was the only time I've ever seen it on you." He paused. "Come to think of it, you weren't wearing it later yesterday, either, were you?"

Russell stepped back, trying to make sense of what his friend George had just said. He didn't even own a Flying Diamonds T-shirt. But if George's memory was faulty, what *did* explain the missing notebook?

The mystery was growing deeper with every passing moment. And Russell knew he'd better unravel it . . . soon!

■ ■ ■ ■

The next day Russell was in the middle of his history class when Ms. Talbott, the principal's assistant, entered and whispered something to his teacher, Ms. Sager. Ms. Sager stopped her lecture on the ancient Egyptians and, looking troubled, turned directly to Russell.

"Russell, Principal Knox would like to see you in his office," she said grimly.

Concerned that he was still being blamed for the missing microscope, Russell quickly gathered up his things and joined Ms. Talbott at the doorway. The woman eyed him scornfully as she ushered him into the hallway.

"What's this about?" Russell asked as they headed down the long hallway to the administration office.

"You'll see," Ms. Talbott replied mysteriously.

A few minutes later Russell found himself standing in Principal Knox's office along with two other boys, both seventh graders. Russell had seen them around school before, but didn't know their names.

"Is this the boy who hit you?" Principal Knox asked the younger boys, indicating Russell.

"Yeah, that's him," said the first boy, a somewhat pudgy kid currently nursing a black eye. "He cornered me near my locker and told me he wanted my wallet. When I wouldn't give it to him, he slugged me."

Russell just stood there in stunned silence. What was this guy talking about?

"He did the same thing to me," said the other kid, a scrawny-looking blond whose broken horn-rimmed glasses were held together with tape. "He beat me up when I wouldn't give him my money."

"Thank you both," the principal said, ushering them to the door. "I'll see that this matter is taken care of."

As the two seventh graders exited, each refused to look Russell in the eye, acting like they were afraid of him. Russell didn't get it. He'd never even spoken to these two kids before in his life!

"Well, Mr. McShane," said Principal Knox, his arms folded across his chest, "what do you have to say for yourself?"

"I—I don't know," Russell stammered. "I never beat up those guys. I don't even know them. This has to be some kind of mistake."

"You know, sometimes successful students get so full of themselves they think they're above the rules. They think they can get away with anything they want," Principal Knox said, his voice oozing with contempt. "That's especially true of star athletes. They think they can break the rules, and no one will challenge them."

"I told you, I didn't beat up those kids!" Russell insisted.

"They identified you both by name and by sight," the principal countered. "Now, don't make things worse by lying, young man."

"I'm not lying!" Russell cried, feeling as though he was living in a nightmare.

"In view of the evidence, I have no choice but to put you on suspension for the next three days," said Principal Knox, taking a seat at his desk. "During this time there will be a full investigation of this matter, after which an appropriate punishment will be determined." He paused, then looked deep into Russell's

11

eyes. "You've disappointed me, Russell. I really thought you were better than this."

Later, on his way home from school, Russell's mind was a jumble of questions. Why was this happening to him? It was almost as if someone was trying to destroy his life. But why?

When he got home, Russell went straight to his bedroom, still concerned with how he was going to tell his parents about his suspension. When he got there, he stopped in horrified shock. His bedroom was a mess—not the normal mess it was usually, but a real mess with drawers opened, clothes strewn all over the place, and books knocked off their shelves.

He was considering the possibility that the entire house had been burglarized when his mother suddenly appeared behind him.

"So you've come back!" she said angrily. "Well? Do you want to explain this?"

"I—I think we must have been robbed," was all Russell could manage to stammer.

"You are unbelievable!" his mother exclaimed. "You come home from school an hour early with absolutely no explanation. Then you run straight up here and tear the place apart. After that you storm out of the house, come back fifteen minutes later, and claim that we've been robbed? Really, Russell, what has gotten into you?"

For a few moments Russell just stood there silently, trying to understand what his mother was saying.

"Wait a minute, you mean you think *I* did this?" Russell asked in disbelief.

"Are you saying you didn't?" his mother replied, equally skeptical. "Oh, please! I saw you with my own two eyes!"

Suddenly the answer to this horrifying mystery became crystal clear to Russell. As incredible as it seemed, the solution that just hit him had to be the only rational explanation for all the weirdness that had been happening.

"Mom, you'll have to excuse me," Russell said. Then he pushed his way past his mother and ran back down the stairs.

"Russell McShane, you come back here this instant!" his mother shouted. But Russell was already out the front door and running full speed down the sidewalk. If it meant having to search every inch of town to find who he was looking for, Russell was prepared to do it.

Fifteen minutes later, after running aimlessly through the streets of the town looking for an all-too-familiar face, Russell crossed the Eighth Avenue Bridge. Halfway across, he came to an abrupt halt. There, standing on the pedestrian walkway, was a boy with his exact build. When he turned around to face Russell, he was wearing not only a wicked smile . . . but a Flying Diamonds T-shirt as well. Russell couldn't believe it. There on the Eighth Avenue Bridge stood . . . himself.

"Looking for someone?" his grinning alter ego asked.

"I don't believe this," Russell said, gasping as he tried to catch his breath.

"Believe it, Russell, my man," his identical twin said with a maniacal laugh as he took a step forward. "I am you. You are me. We are a fam-il-y!"

Since he'd been old enough to talk, Russell McShane knew he had been adopted. It was something his parents had never tried to hide from him. In fact, they always said that being adopted meant he was special. "We wanted you," they'd always told him. "We picked you out of all the others."

But while they had freely revealed his true origins, they'd never said he had a twin brother. For that is what this exact double—this *doppelganger*—certainly was.

"What's your name?" Russell asked, now truly curious.

13

"They call me Jeff Crow, but who knows what my real name is," Russell's double said with a cold grin. "For the past thirteen years, I've been shoved around to so many orphanages and foster homes, who knows *who* I really am?"

"How did you find me?" Russell asked anxiously. "And what do you want?"

"I ran away from my last foster home two months ago," Jeff replied, taking another step forward. "But not before I read my case files. After that, it wasn't hard to track down your family, especially with a star athlete like you in it. I mean, your name's been in the paper a lot lately, Mr. Big Shot Soccer Star." Jeff smiled bitterly. "Fact is, Russell, I've been watching you for over a month—at home, at school—everywhere. You have a wonderful life, Russell. You have a great house. Parents who love you. Friends to hang out with. You have all the things I've never had."

"I'm sorry," Russell said softly. "I didn't know. Really, I had no idea you even existed."

"It's all right, brother," said Jeff, now standing just inches away from him. "Because, beginning right now, I'm going to have everything you have. In fact, I'm going to *be* you!"

And with that, Jeff lunged toward Russell and grabbed him by the throat. Startled, Russell fell against the guard rail and tried to fight back, but Jeff's grip was too strong.

"I wanted you to suffer for a while, to see what it's like to be an outcast," Jeff hissed as he tightened his grip on Russell's throat. "That's why I stole that microscope and framed you for the crime. That's why I beat up those seventh graders and wrecked your room. I wanted you to go through what I've been going through all my life. I wanted you to know how it feels to have everyone hate your guts."

15

Russell balled his right hand into a fist and slammed it into Jeff's side, but his twin didn't budge, keeping his fingers locked around Russell's windpipe.

"Now that I've had my fun, I'm going to replace you," Jeff went on. "I'll give back the microscope and apologize to those seventh-grade geeks. Oh, yes, and I'll clean up your room. Then I'll move in, and your folks and I can be one big happy family."

Russell continued to struggle as hard as he could, but he could tell that Jeff was a lot stronger than he was. Slowly he felt his strength draining out of him and his knees growing weak as his lungs struggled for air.

"Sorry it has to be this way, brother," Jeff said sadly. "But there can only be one Russell McShane . . . and that's going to be *me!*"

Just then a large tanker truck roared by, shaking the bridge beneath the two boys. For a moment Jeff lost his grip, and Russell immediately fell to the asphalt pavement.

Roaring with rage, Jeff leaped toward him, but as he did, Russell jammed his strong, soccer-trained legs straight out, catching Jeff squarely in the chest. Instantly Jeff was knocked against the guard rail, where he lost his balance, flailed for a moment, then fell screaming over the side of the bridge.

Gasping hoarsely, Russell struggled to his feet, scrambled to the railing, and looked down. There he saw only the rushing waters of the river below. His brother, Jeff Crow, was nowhere to be found.

■ ■ ■ ■

Russell McShane immediately reported the encounter and murder attempt to the local police. Their records showed

16

that, indeed, he did have a twin brother named Jeff Crow and that the boy had disappeared from a foster home several weeks earlier. However, even after dragging the river for an entire day, no sign of the boy's body was found.

In the nights that followed, Russell sat in his bed staring out his window wondering what had happened to the twin brother he'd only met for a brief instant. Part of him missed Jeff and wished they could have gotten to know each other under better circumstances. But most of all, Russell was just glad that Jeff was dead . . . probably.

A shiver ran through Russell. He knew there was the slight possibility that Jeff had survived the fall. With that thought in mind, he walked over to his bedroom window and made sure it was locked tight. Jeff was right when he'd said that there is room for only one Russell McShane in this world. And Russell McShane knew that if Jeff was still alive, *he* was going to try to be that one Russell McShane.

deadman's curve

I t was the turning point of her life. This single second, this mere tick of a clock, this insignificant blip on the face of time, would forever seal her fate. Whatever had been—and whatever was to be—all came down to this tenth minute of the eleventh hour of the twentieth day of the third month of her thirteenth year.

Brenda Crane's eyes were shut tight. She could stand the suspense no more. She opened her eyes and looked at the paper clutched in her trembling hands. There, in the same ruby-red ink Mrs. Pavlik always used to grade her math papers, was a quarter-sized circle. And within that circle, smiling up at her like a long-lost friend, was the number "100."

Brenda had done it. All those afternoons of study. Those evenings of practice. The struggle. The anxiety. They had all paid off. She had aced Mrs. Pavlik's algebra midterm.

Even the allergies from which Brenda had been suffering these past few weeks couldn't dampen her excitement as she bounded down the crowded school hallway toward her locker. The midterm counted for a full third of the semester's final grade, and since her homework and weekly quizzes averaged in the 95- to 97-point range, she was now all but assured a solid A, even if she somehow managed to screw up the final. This just about guaranteed her straight A's for the semester.

But before Brenda got to her locker, her pace slowed and her smile dropped. Her best friend, Leslie Finkel, was standing by her own locker looking like a girl about to face a firing squad. Brenda could see the tears welling up in Leslie's eyes. She blew it! Brenda thought, barely managing to keep the smile from creeping back onto her face. She probably got a 95 or even a 90!

As she walked up to Leslie, Brenda tried to think of a way to be diplomatic without sounding overly modest. But before she had a chance to say anything, Leslie handed Brenda her midterm. It was a 67—a D.

Brenda stood in silent shock. This is impossible, she thought. Leslie is one of the smartest girls in school. The worst grade she's ever gotten in her whole life is a B. Still unable to believe it, Brenda was unable to speak. It had taken almost all the energy she could muster just to keep up with Leslie. What could have happened?

Finally Brenda found her voice. "It's got to be a mistake. Maybe Mrs. Pavlik had temporary insanity while she was grading your paper or something."

Leslie shook her head tearfully.

"I—I just couldn't think of the answers," Leslie managed to choke out. "I sat there looking at the problems and all of a sudden I just blanked. Nothing made sense. I feel so . . . stupid!"

"Hey, it's OK, Les," Brenda said, putting a comforting arm around her friend's shoulder. "We all choke sometimes. It's the pressure. It happens."

Again Leslie shook her head. "It's not just the pressure," she insisted. "After class I looked at the test again. I still don't understand it. The stuff I studied all week—it's all mixed up. It's like I'm forgetting everything I ever learned!"

A chill ran down Brenda's spine as she thought of her grandmother who had died just the year before. Over the last two years of her life, the poor woman's mind had slowly slipped away. At first she forgot people's names. Then she forgot who people were. By the end she didn't even know who she was or where she lived. Brenda's parents had explained to her that her grandmother had Alzheimer's disease, which was making her mind deteriorate. They also said that there was no cure.

Could Leslie have Alzheimer's disease? Brenda wondered. But she's only thirteen!

Suddenly Jerry McGuire, the class goofball, interrupted her thoughts like an annoying fly. "Hey, girls, what's happening!" he yelled as he walked toward the lockers.

Jerry always acted like he wasn't smart, but Brenda knew he was. After all, his father was an actual scientist, for crying out loud, and Brenda was convinced that Jerry could be an A-student if he tried. But between his video games, comic books, and TV shows, the best Jerry ever managed was what he called a "Gentleman's C."

Now he was standing in front of Leslie and Brenda, beaming and holding up his midterm. "How'd you two do?" he asked, grinning like a baboon.

"I got a hundred," Brenda replied proudly.

"And how about you, Finkel?" Jerry probed, as if he already knew the awful truth.

"Why, Jerry?" Brenda intervened, hoping to save her friend the embarrassment. "What did you get?"

"A 78," he said flatly. "B-minus."

"A 78 is a C-plus," Brenda corrected him.

"Not on *this* test," Jerry quickly reminded her. "Remember, Mrs. Pavlik grades on a curve."

Jerry was right. Their teacher had explained "the curve" earlier in the year. It was a classic "bell curve," shaped like an upside-down soup bowl, with the few top grades at one end, the few worst grades at the other end, and the "average" grades stacked up in the middle.

Grading using the curve meant that you could do poorly on a test and still get a passing grade . . . as long as everyone else did even worse. So, with Leslie having pulled only a 67, Jerry's 78 became that much more impressive.

"Well, congratulations, Jerry," Brenda said, smiling as she pulled Leslie away. "We're both very proud of you." Brenda took Leslie's arm and was about to lead her away when Jerry pulled her back.

"By the way, I just bought this new breath spray," he said, pulling out a small gray spray bottle. "Tell me what you think."

Before Brenda could object, Jerry shot a cloud of the minty spray straight into her face.

"Achoo!" Brenda sneezed. Immediately her nose began to run and her eyes watered as her allergies kicked in at warp speed. "I hate when you do things like that!" she snapped. "What a creep!"

Again she took Leslie's arm and headed down the hall. As they hurried away, Brenda could hear Jerry laugh. It was just like him, always finding some new twisted way to irritate her. He knew she had allergies, and he probably got some sick kick out of watching her face puff up like a Macy's Thanksgiving Day Parade balloon.

She turned to Leslie, who continued to look depressed.

"Don't worry, Les," Brenda said, plastering a supportive-best-friend smile on her face. "This test was a goof. A fluke. Next time you'll do great."

But Leslie didn't do great the next time. One week later Mrs. Pavlik gave a pop quiz that Leslie should have aced without even breaking a sweat. Instead she got a 58. The next test was even worse—she got a 50!

And Leslie wasn't the only one having trouble. Danny Falk, one of Mrs. Pavlik's top students, suddenly started getting C's and D's. Matt Fong, computer-nerd extraordinaire, watched his scores drop from 95 down to 62. Even Mary Sue Vanderhayden, who was so quick with numbers she'd earned the nickname "The Walking Calculator," flunked two math tests in a row. In fact, Brenda was the only A-student whose grades weren't taking a nosedive.

"I know what's going on," Mrs. Pavlik told her struggling math students. "I've seen it happen before. You A-students are getting lazy. You've always done well before, so you think you can just sit back and coast." She shook her finger at the class. "Well, you can't. Eighth-grade algebra is hard. It takes work. Real work. You're just going to have to buckle down and study."

And that's just what Brenda did. She buckled down and studied. She worked on problems until she thought her fingers would break off. She studied until she felt like her brain was going to explode. And when the next test's grades came back, she got a 97—a solid A.

Leslie and the others weren't as lucky. For the first time in her life, Leslie Finkel actually got an F.

"This can't be an accident," Brenda told Leslie over lunch. It was exactly four weeks to the day since Leslie's first disastrous math midterm. "There's got to be a reason why everyone's grades

23

are going down. Maybe there's something in the water. Or maybe someone is slipping some kind of poison into our food."

"Huh?" Leslie turned to Brenda with a glazed look. Lately it had been harder and harder for Brenda to have an intelligent conversation with her old friend. Leslie's mind always seemed to wander aimlessly, or she'd become totally fixated on something trivial like a shiny piece of jewelry or a glowing sunbeam.

"I'm telling you, this just isn't natural!" Brenda insisted. "Someone—or something—is making the smart kids stupid!"

"How could someone do that?" Leslie asked, barely paying attention. It seemed to take every ounce of her concentration just to eat her tuna fish sandwich.

"I don't know," Brenda admitted, wiping her runny nose. Her allergies had been abating now that spring was almost over, but they still acted up occasionally. "There's got to be a pattern. Some linking element. Let's think—what do all the people affected have in common?"

Leslie shrugged. "I don't know. They all go to school?"

"Besides that," Brenda said with exasperation. She was desperate to find an answer. What if this recent outbreak of "stupid-itis" started to affect *her*?

Brenda was just about to work herself into a real state of panic when she looked up to see Jerry accosting Charlene Cosnofsky, one of the best students in Mr. Mitchell's American history class. Poor Charlene was looking for a place to sit down, and Jerry was pestering her with that same little bottle of breath spray he'd accosted Brenda with earlier. Charlene pushed Jerry away. Then Jerry headed out of the cafeteria, laughing to himself.

"Boy, that guy is so lame," Brenda muttered. "Usually it's rubber vomit, plastic spiders, or fake snakes that jump out of peanut-brittle cans. Now it's some stupid breath spray." She turned to Leslie for a reaction. But her friend was very busy watching an ant crawl across the lunch table.

"Cool," Leslie said.

"Cool? Is that all you can say?" Brenda asked. And then she saw Jerry corner science whiz Eileen Flannagan and spray a puff of his stupid breath freshener in her face.

And then it hit Brenda! Jerry was behind all this with his "breath spray"! Hadn't he tried to spray her—a top student— just like he'd sprayed Charlene and Eileen—also top students?

So why didn't I go stupid when he sprayed me? she thought, absentmindedly rubbing her nose, which caused her to sneeze. "That's it!" she exclaimed. "My allergies! If it wasn't for my stupid stuffed-up nose, I'd be stupid, too!"

She grabbed hold of Leslie's shoulders. "Les, listen to me. About four weeks ago, just before the math midterm, did Jerry spray you with anything?"

All Leslie had to say was, "Huh?" and Brenda had her answer.

■ ■ ■ ■

After school Brenda decided to follow Jerry to see if he'd give himself away. Maybe she'd discover the source of his diabolical power before he could do any more harm . . . and before it was too late to save herself.

But nothing in Jerry's behavior proved to be surprising. His first stop immediately after school was a nearby fast-food restaurant, where he treated himself to a burger and fries. His next stop was the video arcade, where he dropped close to ten dollars worth of quarters in a Cosmic Thunder video game. From there he went to the park, where he shot hoops with three of his goof-off buddies.

25

It wasn't until six o'clock that evening that Jerry finally peddled his bicycle up the driveway of his family's two-story home on Ash Avenue. His father must have arrived earlier, because his car was already parked in the driveway.

"Well, that's it for tonight," Brenda told herself. "No answers here."

She was just about to head home when she noticed an unusual object hanging from the rearview mirror of Jerry's father's car. Curious, Brenda pushed her bike up the driveway to give herself a better view. It was a parking permit. Nothing strange there . . . until Brenda took a closer look. The permit said: WEST TECH LABS—LEVEL 5.

Brenda knew West Tech Labs was a collection of buildings hidden behind a wall of trees on the outskirts of town. She had heard rumors that West Tech did top-secret work for the Army. Does Jerry's dad work for the government? she wondered.

Turning away from the car, Brenda saw a light burning in a far basement window. Moving as inconspicuously as she could, she hurried across the lawn and knelt behind a large bush, from which she had a clear view of the McGuire basement.

Jerry was there. He had a penknife in his hand and was using it to open the lock of a box bearing the name West Tech Labs and a label reading: WARNING: TOXIC. Brenda watched in awe as Jerry opened the mysterious box. Inside, packed in custom-molded foam, were a dozen of the same small gray "breath-spray" containers Jerry had brought to school.

This, Brenda was now certain, was no breath spray.

Excited by her discovery, she ran back across the yard, hopped on her bike, and peddled as fast as she could to Leslie's house four blocks away.

But as she approached the house, Brenda saw two police cars and an ambulance parked out front, their emergency lights flashing. Mrs. Finkel was standing in the front yard, crying as a uniformed police officer tried to comfort her.

Something's wrong with Leslie! Brenda's mind screamed. She threw down her bike and ran up to Mrs. Finkel.

"Where's Leslie?" Brenda demanded. "Is she all right?"

Mrs. Finkel tried to answer but broke down crying. The police officer turned to Brenda gloomily.

"I'm afraid Leslie's dead," the officer reported.

"But—but how?" Brenda cried. "I just saw her at school. She—"

"Apparently she wandered into the street and was hit by a car," the police officer explained. "According to the driver, she didn't even bother to look when she stepped off the curb. I'm sorry. You were a friend of hers?"

"Yes," Brenda replied, bursting into tears. "Leslie was my best friend."

"Was she having trouble at school?" the officer asked. "Was she having problems of any kind?"

You bet she was having problems, Brenda wanted to scream. She was just about to tell the police officer everything, but then she stopped herself. Who was going to believe a story about a spray that makes people stupid?"

"Uh, yeah," she finally said to the officer. "Leslie's grades were slipping. She used to be a top student, and it was really upsetting her."

"Well," the officer said, writing something in her notepad, "maybe her mind was somewhere else when it should have been on the traffic."

Brenda almost laughed. You bet her mind was somewhere else, she thought. In fact, her mind was gone!

That night Brenda considered telling her parents about what she had discovered. But she figured they'd think she was crazy. Besides, she had to be sure her theory was right before she dragged any adults into this. And the best way to do that was to get a confession, a confession from the person she believed caused Leslie to walk in front of that car—Jerry McGuire.

■ ■ ■ ■

The next morning Brenda went looking for Jerry and found him hanging out by his locker. He was showing two of his friends a new noise he'd learned to make with his armpit.

"Excuse me, gentlemen," Brenda said, walking up to the boys. "I don't mean to interrupt this concert, but I really must speak with Mister McGuire—alone."

"Wow, *Mister* McGuire, is it?" one of Jerry's buddies teased. "Does *Mister* McGuire have a girlfriend?"

"Why don't you guys scram?" Jerry said, then he turned to Brenda. "I'll deal with Miss Smarty-Pants, then catch up with you at lunch."

As soon as Jerry's friends were out of earshot, Brenda launched right into Jerry. "I know what you're doing," she said.

"Yeah, it's called making music," Jerry said, laughing as he pumped his armpit a few more times.

"I mean I know what you're doing with that spray," Brenda continued without a trace of a smile. "You're a C-student. You wanted better grades, and you weren't willing to work for them. So you figured you'd make yourself look smarter by making the really smart people stupid."

"And how could I do that?" Jerry asked matter-of-factly.

"Your father is a government scientist," Brenda stated. "I don't know all the details, but I can guess he's been working on a chemical that slows down the brain. It would be the perfect

28

weapon. What better way to win a war than to turn the enemy into idiots?"

Jerry looked around furtively to see if anyone was listening.

"Anyway," Brenda went on not skipping a beat, "you got hold of a sample and have been spraying everyone whose grades were better than yours. When everyone else's grades went down, yours went up. Thanks to the curve."

"That's an interesting theory." Jerry smiled. "You're really smart. Too smart. What I can't figure out is why this didn't work the first time!" And with that Jerry whipped out his "breath spray," and before she could react, Brenda felt a cool, minty mist hit her squarely in the face.

But this time she didn't sneeze! This morning, without thinking, she had taken some new allergy pills her mother had bought for her . . . and now she could breathe perfectly.

"You're not going to get away with this!" Brenda screamed, even as the spray's sweet scent filled her nostrils. And with that she turned and marched straight for the principal's office. The last she saw of Jerry, he was still standing by his locker . . . laughing.

Still enraged, Brenda stormed into Principal Turner's office. A tall red-haired woman, Principal Turner looked up curiously from her desk. "Brenda?" she inquired with surprise. "What's wrong? You look upset."

"It's about Jerry McGuire," Brenda began. "He's—"

"Has he been making trouble again?" Principal Turner asked with obvious irritation. "He's already been in here three times this month for pulling practical jokes."

"It's worse than that," Brenda said. "He's got this . . . this thing!"

"What thing?" asked Principal Turner.

"You know, this thing. He . . . he's got . . ." Brenda

stammered. She shook her head as if trying to clear it. What was wrong with her? Why couldn't she find the right words?

"Now, just calm down," Principal Turner said softly. "Sit down and tell me just what Jerry did."

Brenda took a seat and tried to concentrate. But she didn't feel like herself. Her eyes began to wander. She looked up at the framed certificates hanging above Principal Turner's desk. They were all written in fancy script she knew she should be able to read but for some reason she just couldn't.

"Brenda?" Principal Turner looked at her with concern. "Are you all right?"

Brenda looked at the principal blankly. What had she just been thinking? She couldn't remember. And why had she come here in the first place? It had something to do with . . . what was his name?

"Brenda, I'm very busy right now." Principal Turner's voice was becoming stern. "If you have something to say, please say it."

"Sorry," Brenda said vacantly. Her eyes glazing over, Brenda walked slowly out of Principal Turner's office. Without purpose, without direction, she wandered down the crowded hallway, through the front doors, and out into the bright sunlight.

Without thinking where she was or what she was doing, Brenda strolled out into the busy street in front of her junior high school. She heard a loud, insistent honk and turned to see the front of a late-model minivan speeding toward her.

Wow! Brenda thought. Cool.

public enemy

_____

As soon as the SOLD sign went up in front of the old Robinson house across Euclid Street, Paul Potter became suspicious. The place was a dump. It always had been. The single-story clapboard home's dingy brown paint hadn't been retouched in at least twenty years. Over half the asphalt shingles were missing from its sagging roof. Several broken windowpanes had been haphazardly covered with yellowed newspaper, and the lawn was completely overgrown with wild grass and prickly weeds.

"Anyone who'd buy that house would have to be crazy," Paul's father had declared upon Old Man Robinson's death more than two years before. "It's a disaster area. A black hole. Only a nutcase would want to live in that house!"

31

And, in fact, the house *had* gone unsold for over two years. Some of the neighborhood kids insisted that the house was haunted. Some said that anyone who stayed there overnight would have his or her heart ripped out by the ghost of Old Man Robinson himself! Of course, as far as Paul knew, no one had tried to sleep there—but if anyone had, Paul had no doubt that he or she would have suffered some unspeakably grisly fate.

Then one fateful Friday in late September, a real-estate agent had appeared on the lawn of the old Robinson house and plastered a SOLD sign over the graffiti-covered FOR SALE sign. Clearly the residents of Euclid Street were about to have a new neighbor moving in.

"Who would ever buy that house?" Paul wondered out loud to his best friend, Nick Lorenzo, who lived three doors down.

"Maybe a vampire who's looking for a little privacy," Nick speculated. He tended to be overly imaginative, and no one ever took him very seriously. "Or a ghoul who doesn't want anyone seeing him feasting on human flesh."

"Yeah, right. Or maybe a mad scientist bought the place," Paul chimed in. "And he's making a monster in his basement." Of course, Paul knew this was impossible. The old Robinson place didn't even have a basement.

The guessing game continued throughout the afternoon. Whoever the mysterious buyer was, Paul and Nick figured he or she was either a notorious gangster, an escaped mental patient, an international terrorist, an exotic spy, or the leader of an alien invasion force.

They agreed to keep an eye on the house from their bedrooms, which between them provided a 160-degree range of visual coverage. They would each take one-hour shifts, with time off for sleep, school, meals, homework, and TV. With luck, they'd soon know if their new neighbor was friend or foe.

Their first big break in the case of the mysterious neighbor happened during Paul's seven o'clock Monday morning shift. Actually Paul wasn't observing the Robinson house at the time. He was getting dressed for school. It was only by accident that he happened to glance out his bedroom window while throwing on his shirt. That's when he saw a beat-up pickup truck pulling up in front of the Robinson house. In its flatbed area were a half-dozen large cardboard boxes and a black tarpaulin. Nothing more.

Bursting with excitement, Paul grabbed the binoculars he'd gotten the previous Christmas, ran to the window, and focused his attention on the street below. His heart pounding, he watched breathlessly as the truck's door opened and a large man stepped out.

Instantly Paul sensed trouble. This guy was huge—at least six feet ten inches tall—and seemingly half as wide as he was tall. He had big, bulging arms to match his equally big, bulging belly. He had a buzz haircut, wore a heavy metal band T-shirt and torn blue jeans, and looked like he hadn't shaved—or bathed—in a week.

As Paul continued to watch through his binoculars, the giant man reached into the back of his truck and picked up one of the big cardboard boxes. He took a few steps toward the old Robinson house, and then, as if sensing he was being watched, he slowly turned back, looked up . . . and stared straight at Paul.

Now Paul had been scared before—like when he went into the hospital to get his tonsils out, or when he belly-flopped off the high dive at camp. But nothing in Paul's entire thirteen years had felt anything like the cold, clammy, chilled-to-the-bone terror that flashed down his spine as his eyes locked with those of his new neighbor. Looking into those eyes was like peering into a bottomless pit, an abyss of sheer, ice-cold nothingness.

And then the man smiled. It was the kind of smile a spider might give a fly before snuffing out its pathetic little life. Or the kind of smile a shark might flash a tuna just before wrapping its iron jaws around its prey's flailing fish flesh.

Paul jumped away from the window, tossed the binoculars onto his bed, and bolted from the bedroom. In the hallway he nearly slammed into his father, who was already dressed and heading down to breakfast.

"Whoa! Slow down, big guy!" his father admonished him. "What's your hurry?"

"Nothing," Paul squeaked. How do you tell your dad that the guy who just moved in across the street is a homicidal maniac?

■ ■ ■ ■

A few days later word was out that Paul's new neighbor was named Martin Childers and that he had just moved into town from somewhere on the East Coast. No one knew what he did for a living, but it was obvious that whatever it was, it didn't involve going to an office. In fact, Childers rarely seemed to venture out of his house, and when he did he usually looked like he'd just spent the last forty-eight hours sleeping in a pile of dirty laundry. His face was always stubbled and his clothes always looked like castoffs from the local homeless shelter. But what bothered Paul most about Childers was his look. It was a mean, cut-the-throat-of-anyone-who-looked-at-him-sideways look, a look that chilled Paul's soul.

At first Paul thought he'd never get over having a creep like that living next door to him. But as the days and weeks passed, he started to get used to the man's odd appearance and irregular comings and goings. In fact, Paul probably would

34

have forgotten about Childers altogether if he hadn't caught a particular episode of his all-time favorite TV show, *Public Enemy*.

That evening, as Paul expected, he saw the show's customary true-to-life accounts of vicious killers, kidnappers, bank robbers, and other assorted criminal scum who were still wanted by various law enforcement agencies across the country. The program included the usual "dramatic reenactment" of each criminal's crime, as well as the photos and bios of the real-life criminals who were still at large.

But what Paul didn't expect to see was his new neighbor, Martin Childers, presented as the show's "Public Enemy Number One." True, the man on the TV wasn't named Childers—his name was George Jerome Throckmorton, otherwise known as the "Slice-and-Dice Killer." But that was no big deal. Paul just figured Childers had been giving everyone on Euclid Street a phony name. After all, didn't criminals always use an alias to hide from the cops? Childers probably had a dozen aliases.

Another difference was that George Jerome Throckmorton had long, stringy hair. But Paul knew that for ten bucks the man could have gotten his current buzz cut at any barber shop in town. And so what if George Jerome Throckmorton was a good two inches shorter than Childers and only weighed about two hundred pounds. Paul figured that Childers simply wore elevator shoes and put on the extra fifty pounds by eating a lot or by strapping on fake padding.

No, it wasn't the photo or the description of George Jerome Throckmorton that made Paul sure the two men were one and the same. It was the man's eyes.

Yes, those cold, black, plunge-a-dagger-into-your-very-soul eyes convinced Paul Potter beyond a shadow of a doubt that Martin Childers was indeed the dreaded Slice-and-Dice

Killer. No two human beings could have eyes as dark and chilling as those.

Paul always videotaped *Public Enemy*. He never knew when his teacher, the pharmacist, or in this case, his neighbor, would turn out to be a wanted fugitive. As a result, he had his evidence in hand when his father naturally dismissed his charge against the mysterious man next door as pure fantasy.

"But I'm sure of it, Dad!" Paul insisted, pointing to the face of George Jerome Throckmorton locked in freeze-frame on the family-room TV. "Mr. Childers just changed his appearance to fool the police. Come on, look at those eyes. He could change everything else, but he couldn't change his eyes!"

"Paul, I agree that Mr. Childers is an odd fellow, but I assure you, he's not the Slice-and-Dice Killer," his father said with calm certainty. "Serial killers don't live on nice, normal suburban streets like ours."

Paul nearly screamed with frustration. He wanted to tell his father that he was wrong, that that's exactly where serial killers live—on nice, normal suburban streets like their own. But Paul knew better than to argue with his father. The man was a certified public accountant. He had been trained to deal with cold, hard numbers, not the irrational, often wholly insane passions that drove people like Childers. No, if Martin Childers, a.k.a. the Slice-and-Dice Killer, was going to be brought to justice, he, Paul Potter, would have to do it himself . . . maybe with a little help from his friend.

■ ■ ■ ■

"Shhhh! Be careful!" Paul whispered to Nick as they slowly crept across Euclid Street toward the old Robinson house. "He's probably inside watching the street, looking for cops."

37

Paul clutched his camera in his sweaty, trembling hands. With every step he took, he mentally computed the time necessary to retreat to the safety of his house should Childers bolt from the front door brandishing one of his dreaded knives. The way Paul figured it, every step that he and Nick took toward the creepy old house diminished their chances of a successful escape by at least ten percent. And once they actually set foot on Childers's property, Paul guessed the odds were better than even that either he or his friend—and maybe both of them— would fall victim to a deadly blade before they could get away.

"Here," Paul whispered, handing Nick the camera. "You take a picture of the license plate while I keep a lookout."

Nick squatted and obediently clicked off two shots of the pickup truck's New York license plate.

"Now come around this way and get a couple of shots," Paul instructed, waving Nick toward the truck's flatbed cargo section.

Nick hurried over and again clicked off two photos.

Holding his breath, afraid of what he might uncover, Paul pulled back the heavy plastic tarpaulin that was crumpled in the corner. Below it were several large, dark brown stains. "Th-that looks like dried blood," he stammered. "Quick, get a picture of it!"

"Looks more like dried *mud* to me," Nick said, unconsciously shivering. Still, he took a quick shot of it.

After a few more pictures of the flatbed, the boys moved to the truck's cab. Again they saw several dark, brownish stains, this time on the upholstered passenger seat.

"Maybe he was drinking coffee and spilled it," Nick ventured with forced optimism.

"Yeah, and maybe he's a vampire and he dripped blood from his fangs," Paul said sarcastically. "No—this is probably where Childers kills his victims. Then he throws them in the back of the truck, covers them with the tarp, and takes them somewhere to bury them."

At Paul's insistence, Nick snapped off three pictures of the mystery stains on the truck's front seat. Then, together, they made a slow, careful approach around the dilapidated house to its overgrown backyard.

"I wouldn't be surprised if there were a dozen bodies buried right back here," Paul said. "Come on. Let's see."

Despite his own prediction, no one was more surprised than Paul when they rounded the corner of the house and saw that half of the yard's weed garden had been cleared away. In its place were six mounds of freshly dug earth, each approximately six feet long and two feet wide.

"They—they look like . . . graves," Nick stammered.

"Shoot pictures of them!" Paul ordered excitedly.

But Nick was too scared to move, obviously paralyzed by the thought of what might be lying beneath those six mounds of freshly dug earth.

"Give me that thing!" Paul said, grabbing the camera from his friend's trembling hands. He shot four more pictures from various angles and was about to return the camera to Nick when he saw that his friend's gaze had become fixed on the old Robinson house. Slowly—very slowly—Paul turned to see what had so captivated his friend's attention.

There, staring at them through a dusty window no more than fifteen feet away, was the snarling, hate-filled face of Martin Childers.

Paul was the first to scream, and as screams go, it was one of the all-time best. It was loud, long, and strong, and it could have given any police siren a run for its money. Nick's scream wasn't too shabby, either. It sounded like some kind of primal howl.

Together the terrified boys sprinted away from the house out onto Euclid Street, then up Paul's front walk, and through his front door, slamming and bolting it behind them.

"We got him!" Paul gasped, waving the camera in front of Nick's still-petrified face. "We got him good!"

■ ■ ■ ■

Paul and Nick didn't even bother to shoot off the rest of the twenty-four-frame film cartridge. Instead they took it straight to the nearest one-hour photo developing store, and in just over an hour they had their evidence in hand.

"Who do we take them to?" Nick asked, thumbing through the photos.

"We should call the *Public Enemy* hotline," Paul suggested, referring to the 24-hour toll-free number viewers were asked to call with their tips.

"What can a TV show do?" Nick wanted to know. "We have to take this evidence straight to the police."

Nick was right, and Paul knew it. His neighbor was a crazed killer who could strike at any moment. The police had to be notified immediately.

■ ■ ■ ■

The detectives' squad room was a lot smaller than the ones Paul had seen on TV. There were only four desks, three file cabinets, and one counter with a small coffee machine on it and the remnants of a few donuts. Paul looked around the room, disappointed that he didn't see any WANTED posters lying around.

"Boys, this is Detective Warner," said the desk sergeant who had been the first officer they'd met when they entered the police station. "Detective, this is Paul Potter and Nick Lorenzo. They have something they want to show you."

Paul handed over the photographs and told Detective Warner about his notorious neighbor, the *Public Enemy* show he'd seen, and their terrible discoveries in Childers's truck and backyard.

Detective Warner, sitting back in his chair, listened to every word, and when Paul was finished, he leaned forward and smiled. "We appreciate your concern, boys," he said. "But I can assure you, this Mr. Childers is not the Slice-and-Dice Killer. It's my guess that the two of you have just let your imaginations take you for a little ride."

"But we have evidence!" Paul insisted, pointing to the photographs. "See that license plate? Childers is from New York! *Public Enemy* said the Slice-and-Dice Killer was last seen in New York."

"New York's a big state," Detective Warner said calmly.

"And look at these bloodstains in the back of his truck," Paul pressed on, shoving the next picture into the officer's face.

"Looks like mud to me," Detective Warner said flatly.

"Does this look like mud?" Paul challenged, showing the detective his picture of the truck's stained front seat.

"No, it doesn't look like mud." Detective Warner grinned. "It looks like spilled coffee."

"Well, if Childers isn't a serial killer, then how do you explain the six freshly dug graves in his backyard?" Paul demanded, fixing the detective with a determined stare.

"Maybe your neighbor is just doing some planting," Detective Warner replied, getting up. "Now, look, boys, I've got a lot of work to do."

Nick finally spoke up. "OK, maybe we're wrong," he said. "But shouldn't you at least check it out? I mean, even if there's a chance we're right?"

Detective Warner smiled. "I know Mr. Childers isn't the Slice-and-Dice Killer because the FBI arrested him last night out in Eugene, Oregon." He walked over and shook Paul's hand, then Nick's. "But, like I said, we appreciate your concern. We need sharp-eyed citizens like you watching the streets. Keep up the good work."

With that he turned away from the boys and left the room.

■ ■ ■ ■

Paul's father was livid when he heard what his son had done. "You owe Mr. Childers an apology," he said, a stern look on his face. "You trespassed on his property. You accused him of a horrible crime. And then you took up the valuable time of a police detective." He paced the room, obviously deciding Paul's fate. "Now, I want you to march over to Mr. Childers's house right now and tell him you're sorry. And then I want you to write a letter of apology to Detective Warner."

Paul wanted to protest, but he knew that once his father got an idea into his head, it was there for good. Besides, it did kind of look like he'd made a mistake. After all, Detective Warner had said they'd already arrested the wanted murderer.

So, with his head bowed, Paul walked slowly across Euclid Street, up Childers's cracked asphalt driveway right to his rotting front doorstep. He didn't want to knock on the door for fear of catching some sort of horrible fungal disease, but he forced himself to do it anyway. If my hand dries up and falls off, he thought as his knuckles hit the diseased wood, it will be all Dad's fault.

"Who is it?" a voice bellowed hoarsely from inside not two seconds after Paul knocked.

"Paul Potter, your neighbor," Paul responded, his voice quivering. "I—I live across the street."

Paul heard movement inside the house, then the front door opened. A stubbly-chinned Childers stood there wearing his usual uniform of a stained T-shirt and torn jeans. To Paul, he still looked like a killer. And worse, he smelled exactly like a garbage truck.

"Oh, it's you," Childers muttered. "You and your friend were poking around here taking pictures."

"Yes," Paul admitted, "and I just came here to say I'm sorry." He paused for a moment, expecting Childers to either accept his apology or kill him on the spot. "It won't happen again, sir. I promise."

Childers looked Paul up and down, checking him out. "Come on in," he said, disappearing into his house.

Paul hesitated. What was he supposed to do? He couldn't possibly be expected to enter this creepy old place, could he?

"I got some soft drinks here," Childers called over his shoulder. "You like root beer?"

"Uh, sure," Paul found himself saying as he carefully stepped inside.

As Paul had expected, the interior of the place was just as bad as the exterior. There were no carpets on the rotting wooden floors. The ancient wallpaper was peeling off all over the place, and the ceiling was blistering from years of water damage. What little furniture Childers had consisted of two rickety card table chairs, a torn lawn lounger, and a table made from an old wooden crate.

And that smell! How could anyone stand to live in a house with such a stench! It smelled like rotting meat.

Paul looked around as he waited for Childers to return from the kitchen. There were several open boxes in the center of the living room. He stepped closer to peer inside one and saw that it was filled with comic books—old comic books, many of which were classics and quite valuable.

"Wow," Paul murmured. "Cool!"

"You know, I haven't had a chance to meet many of the folks in the neighborhood," Childers called from the other room. "I guess it's my fault, really. I'm kind of shy."

"It's OK," Paul called back. "I know it's tough being the new kid on the block. At least, that's what I've heard."

"So, what were you taking pictures of?" Childers asked, still rummaging around out of sight.

Paul almost laughed out loud. Now he was feeling like a total idiot. "It's really kind of funny," he said. "Last night I was watching a TV show called *Public Enemy*. Do you ever watch it?"

"I don't own a TV," came Childers's reply. "Plus, I usually go out at night."

"Anyway, they had a story on about a guy called the Slice-and-Dice Killer," Paul went on, approaching another box as he talked. It looked just like all the others—square and made of off-white cardboard. Probably full of more cool comics, Paul thought, wondering if Childers would ever trade anything for a few of them. "And they showed a picture of the guy on television," Paul said, feeling a little nervous about going on. "And, well, he kind of looked like—I know this sounds dumb—but the guy kind of looked like you."

"Like me?" Childers asked, his voice rising in surprise.

"Yeah, he kind of did look like you," Paul said, chuckling a little as he reached for the lid of the box. "So my friend Nick and I, we decided to investigate, and that's why we were snooping around." He paused, waiting for a response that never came.

44

"Anyway, we took some pictures and we went to the police. But the detective we spoke to said the killer was already captured." Again he waited for a response, and when he heard nothing, he called out, "Pretty funny, huh?"

Childers made no reply, and shrugging, Paul lifted the lid off the box and peered inside.

All at once his stomach leaped clear up to his throat, and he lost all ability to speak. There were no comics in this box. There were skulls—human skulls! They were piled one on top of the other, their shrunken eyeballs looking like big, wrinkled raisins.

"Yeah, that *is* funny," Childers said, suddenly standing right behind Paul. "*Me*—the Slice-and-Dice Killer. That *is* a laugh . . . especially since I think knives are sloppy. Me—I like chain saws." He paused for a moment. "Like this one," he said, whipping a huge chain saw out from behind his back. He yanked it to life and laughed.

Those were the last two things Paul Potter ever heard—the roar of the chain saw's gasoline engine coming to life to take his own, and Childers's terrible laugh. And the very last thing Paul saw is what chilled him the most—he saw those cold black eyes. Black as night. Black as all eternity.

suspended animation

izzy staggered into the police station, an expression of absolute terror on her face. Moments ago she'd found herself lying under a large boulder. She wasn't hurt, but she certainly felt different. She didn't exactly know how, but for some reason she knew that her entire world had changed. "Sergeant Foxx, you've got to help me!" Lizzy cried.

The sergeant, Felix Foxx, was munching on a powdered donut about the size of a bicycle tire when Lizzy raced up to his cluttered desk.

"Just a second," he said, motioning for Lizzy to take a seat. "Now," he went on, wiping doughnut crumbs off of his chest, "how can I help you?"

"Something is wrong," was all Lizzy could say.

"What do you mean, wrong?" Sergeant Foxx inquired.

"Has there been a murder? A bombing? A theft? Has someone tried to rob the First National Bank? The Second National Bank? The Last National Bank?"

"No, no, no," Lizzy said, shaking her head. "Nothing like that."

"Don't tell me that darn dam has busted!" the police officer shouted, seemingly on the verge of panic. He reached for his telephone, punched in a number, and barked into the mouthpiece. "Call out the Army! The Navy! The Mormon Tabernacle Choir! The dam has burst! The dam has burst!"

Lizzy placed a finger on the phone's cradle, cutting the connection.

"The dam is fine," she said, annoyed that Sergeant Foxx was obviously not taking her seriously.

"Then why are you here?" Sergeant Foxx demanded angrily. "This is a police station. We have serious business to attend to!"

"Pizza delivery!" called a man in the doorway. He looked like an ancient Roman, complete with a laurel and flowing toga.

"Right here," the sergeant said, motioning him over. "Boy, I'm hungry enough to eat a horse!"

"That's not funny!" said the police horse standing in a hay-lined stall located next to the station's single holding cell.

"Sorry," said Sergeant Foxx, looking a little sheepish. Then he quickly turned his attention to the piping hot pizza before him.

Lizzy stared at the horse as it returned to munching its bag of oats. Had that animal just talked? Of course it had. All animals talk. Or do they? Lizzy was confused. This was just the kind of puzzling problem she'd been struggling with all day.

"Wait a minute!" Sergeant Foxx bellowed as the pizza man was heading for the door. "I specifically told you people, *no anchovies!*"

"Sorry about that," the delivery man said apologetically. He placed two fingers in his mouth and made a sound like an old-fashioned factory steam whistle. Immediately the sixteen anchovies on the sergeant's pizza jumped up, flapped their fins, and ran on their little fishtails across the desk. Then they hopped down to the floor and skittered to the entrance where, one by one, they jumped into a pocket that had suddenly appeared on the delivery man's toga.

"There—no anchovies!" the delivery man declared. He then tossed the sergeant a casual salute, turned, and headed out the front door.

"Did you see that!" Lizzy cried, pointing after the delivery man. "That's what I'm talking about!"

"Huh?" Sergeant Foxx grunted, a huge string of pizza cheese hanging out of his mouth.

Lizzie frowned. "Those anchovies jumped off your pizza and into the delivery man's pocket."

"So?" the sergeant said, wearing a blank expression. "I told him I don't like anchovies."

"But fish can't even live on dry land!" Lizzy exclaimed.

"What's your point?" Sergeant Foxx asked impatiently.

"My point is that something is seriously, well, *fishy*!" Lizzy insisted. "Things are happening that shouldn't be happening. And not just here—they're happening everywhere I've been today. For example, when the sun rose this morning it had a big happy face on it!" Lizzy shrugged helplessly. "I mean, I know that these things happen all the time, but suddenly they seem weird—like maybe they aren't normal?"

"What's so strange about that?" the sergeant asked, baffled by her problem. "The sun always smiles. It has a sunny disposition."

"And that's not all," Lizzy went on, completely ignoring him. "As I was getting dressed, I noticed I only had one set of

49

clothes. When I mentioned it to my parents, they told me that *everyone* has only one set of clothes. Don't you think that it's strange that people dress exactly the same way day after day?"

Sergeant Foxx paused just long enough to look down at his police uniform.

"Maybe that's not a good example," Lizzy said dismissively. "But listen to this. When I went to school, I took a good look at all the other kids in my class. I mean a good look. Do you know what I discovered?"

Sergeant Foxx popped the last of his pizza slice into his mouth, then smacked his lips. "Nope," he answered.

"Danny Duck? He's a *duck*!" Lizzy cried. "Benny Bear? He's a *bear*! Katey Kangaroo—?"

Sergeant Foxx raised his gloved hand. "Let me guess. She's a walrus?"

"She's a *kangaroo*!" Lizzy shouted.

"Well, I was close," the sergeant said with a shrug.

"And look at me," Lizzy said. "I'm a lizard! *Lizzy Lizard!* I had no idea how odd I looked until I saw this!" She pulled out a torn piece of paper and showed it to Sergeant Foxx. "I mean, I've got scales and a long skinny tail!"

"Hey, did you tear that out of a school library book?" Sergeant Foxx asked, leaning forward accusingly. "That's destruction of public property!"

"Why can't you understand?" Lizzy moaned. "A lizard shouldn't be going to school! And neither should ducks or bears or kangaroos!"

"I wouldn't advise dropping out," Sergeant Foxx said. He leaned back in his chair and rubbed his full tummy. "A mind is a terrible thing to waste."

"None of this is right. I must be dreaming," Lizzy insisted, looking frantically all around the police station. "Walking fish.

Talking horses. Foxes in police uniforms eating pizza. I don't know why, but it shouldn't be happening. It can't be happening. I have to be dreaming!"

"Look, Lizzy, you're obviously upset," Sergeant Foxx said softly, trying to remain as friendly as possible. "But if anything's wrong around here, I'd say it's you. You say horses can't talk? Henry here might disagree with you."

"Indubitably," said the police horse, suddenly speaking in a highbrow British accent.

"You say ducks and bears and kangaroos shouldn't go to school? They always have, it's the law," the police officer went on. "What would you have them do? Hang out at video arcades? And as for wearing the same clothes every day, I'd say that's a problem for you, your parents, and the fashion police, not this local law enforcement agency."

Lizzy stared at the sergeant's red, furry face, long snout, pointed ears, and shifty brown eyes.

"Forget I ever mentioned anything," she said flatly. Then she picked up her schoolbooks and headed wearily toward the door.

"Hey, thanks for stopping by!" Sergeant Foxx shouted after her, waving vigorously. "Remember, the police are here to protect and to serve!"

Feeling depressed and confused, Lizzy Lizard padded slowly down the station's front steps and out into the bright sunlight, instinctively taking care to avoid any potential areas of shade. Shielding her eyes, she gazed up at the blazing afternoon sun. This being a particularly hot day, the sun itself was now wearing sunglasses. One part of Lizzy still found this perfectly normal, while another side now thought it was absolutely absurd.

How can the sun wear sunglasses? she suddenly wondered. It's a huge, blazing ball of hydrogen gas over ninety million miles away. It's not alive . . . and it doesn't have eyes!

51

Again she looked up at the sun. The sun apparently saw her, for one of its rays took the form of a hand and gave her a little wave.

Shrugging, Lizzy was just about to find a good warm place to sit down and figure out all this weirdness when someone shouted, "Look out below!"

Looking up, Lizzy saw a huge iron safe break loose from a pulley and chain . . . and it was plunging right toward Jazzy Giraffe, who was on the sidewalk playing his saxophone twenty stories below.

"Jazzy!" she screeched. But it was too late. The safe hit the unsuspecting giraffe right on the head, turning its long, thin neck into a pleated accordion that bounced up and down several times making sour musical sounds. Then the giraffe's lanky neck miraculously snapped back to normal.

"Cool, man!" the giraffe intoned, obviously unhurt.

Increasingly frightened and confused by her illogical world, Lizzy stumbled on through town. Everywhere she looked, previously ordinary things seemed more and more absurd. People were being run over by steamrollers only to somehow pop back to life after being squashed as flat as pancakes. Cats chased birds off rooftops, hung in midair for impossible lengths of time, and only when they noticed there was nothing below them, would they go plummeting to the ground. And cars, buses, and even lampposts would take on human faces, then begin acting and breathing like living, animated creatures.

Why am I the only one who thinks this is wrong? Lizzy's mind screamed as she continued to run down Main Street. Why has everyone always regarded this as normal?

Just then, Lizzy stopped short as she slammed head-on into what at first felt like a brick wall. But when she stumbled back, she saw that it wasn't a wall at all. It was more like a gigantic plate of glass. Running her hand along it, she discovered that it ran as high as she could reach and as far to either side as she could run. It was, for all intents and purposes, a huge invisible barrier that separated her and her town from . . . what?

Her heart racing, Lizzy pressed her face against the barrier and tried to peer beyond it. What she saw filled her with terror. She appeared to be gazing into a giant living room. But it was like no room she'd ever seen before. Its colors were dark and muted, not the bright, blazing hues that made up her world. And the furniture—it had more detail to it and was textured rather than smooth and simple like the furniture in her home.

But most frightening of all was how big the room was. In fact, it was downright gigantic. The chairs were the size of mountains. The lamps were taller than the tallest trees in the forest. And the people . . .

"People," she whispered to herself. Yes, that's what those gigantic creatures staring back at her from the other side of the glass were called. Taller than any giant she'd ever encountered, these magnificent beings were . . . humans. And unlike Lizzy or her neighbors, they had solid bodies that didn't stretch or twist like putty. They were, Lizzy realized with great sadness, really alive . . . and she wasn't. Yes, it finally dawned on her that she, Lizzy Lizard, was nothing but a drawing, a colorful toon. An animated character! She wasn't real. And that realization filled her with more fear than she'd ever felt before.

"Wait a minute," she said to herself, trying to sort things out. "If I'm not real, I don't exist. And if I don't exist how can I be thinking this?" Then a lightbulb appeared over her head and started to shine brightly. "That must mean that I *do* exist. I *am* alive. I *am* real!"

Suddenly Lizzy's joy came to a screeching halt as she heard someone on the other side of the glass barrier talking.

"This is the dumbest cartoon I've ever seen in my life," a young boy was saying.

"What's on channel eight?" a young girl asked impatiently.

"I don't know, let's see," the boy said. And with that he reached for the remote control.

Lizzy Lizard saw this and panicked. Her heart leaped into her throat and tears welled up in her eyes.

"No! Don't change the channel!" she shouted. "Don't turn me off! I don't want to die! I want to live!"

A second later there was a click—and Lizzy was gone.

The boy scoffed. "Sometimes cartoons are so stupid."

He was right. A lot of cartoon characters are stupid. But every once in a while a very smart toon comes along.

the foxboro ghost

elanie Claymore's heart sank as the family car paused in the driveway of the big, gloomy stone house that stood on the outskirts of suburban Foxboro, New Jersey. "I can't believe you paid $550,000 for this!" she exclaimed.

"To tell you the truth, sometimes neither can I!" her father confessed. "Come on, let's take a look at our new home."

Melanie and her big brother, Charlie, climbed out of the backseat and followed their parents up the front steps of a large covered porch. But as she approached the big brick house, Melanie kept getting the impression that someone was watching them. Shuddering, she gazed up at the oversize windows, and suddenly it occurred to her—it was the house *itself* that was eyeing them.

That's ridiculous! she told herself. Still, the feeling that the house was watching them made Melanie distinctly uneasy.

"Well, folks, here we are," her father said proudly as he took out his new house key. He carefully opened the deadbolt lock, pushed open the heavy, intricately carved front door, then turned to Melanie's mother, and asked, "Shall I carry you across the threshold, madam?"

"If you insist," her mother replied with a laugh.

"Better hurry up before you pull something, Dad," Melanie offered, seeing her father's face turn red as he lifted her mother and began to carry her through the doorway.

"That's enough out of you," her dad said good-naturedly as he moved awkwardly toward the wide threshold. But as he did, his right foot got caught in a rotted plank, and he nearly tripped before successfully pulling his shoe free. "Hmmm. I'll have to have that fixed," he muttered, then stumbled on, nearly hitting his wife's head on the door frame in the process.

Melanie and Charlie looked at each other, rolling their eyes.

"Parents can be so *weird*," Melanie groaned.

"Tell me about it," Charlie said. He paused. Leaning toward her he lowered his voice as if to share a deep, dark secret. "You know what I heard about this place? It's haunted by the ghost of the gangster who built it back in the 1920s. The guy's name was Alphonse Blaine, and people around here say that one night he caught his girlfriend smooching with one of his bodyguards. Anyway, he got so mad that first he killed the bodyguard, then he killed his girlfriend, and then he killed himself."

"I heard the same thing," Melanie said with a shiver. "And now Blaine's spirit supposedly roams these halls, chasing away anyone who dares to enter his domain."

"Right," Charlie said, "which makes this place a deathtrap. Too bad Dad just spent every penny we have to buy it."

"And it was worth it," their father said, sticking his head back out through the doorway. "I mean, the other fellow sure thought so, didn't he?"

The "other fellow" their father referred to was the rival buyer they'd gotten into a "bidding war" with over the house. As Melanie understood it, the previous owners had initially asked $400,000 for the property, and her parents, who'd just received a sizable inheritance following the death of her father's rich uncle, decided to just offer the full amount. But then this other mystery buyer came along and offered $410,000. Figuring they were still getting a bargain, Melanie's parents upped their offer to $420,000. By the time the back-and-forth bidding was over, her parents had emerged the "winners"—paying $150,000 more for the house than the astonished owners had originally asked for.

"It's a good investment," Melanie's dad had explained. "In ten years, it'll be worth *twice* that. Obviously the guy who was bidding against us believed that, right?"

So here they were, the proud owners of a fifteen-room house, a half-acre of land, a detached three-car garage . . . and a killer ghost.

■ ■ ■ ■

That first night Melanie went to bed amidst a virtual obstacle course of unpacked suitcases and boxes. It had taken her nearly a month to pack up all the clothes, books, stuffed animals, and games from her old bedroom, and she figured it would take her at least that long to unpack them all now. She'd just started the process when she began to wonder if it was even worth the effort. The ghost would probably chase her family away before she'd finished unpacking her first suitcase.

Although she was already thirteen years old, Melanie saw no reason *not* to believe in ghosts. After all, she knew for certain that she was more than just a bunch of organs and bones. She also knew that she had a soul or a spirit, and it made sense that a person's spirit could live on long after his or her flesh-and-blood body had died and rotted away. The way Melanie figured it, if a person died under sudden or violent circumstances, like the way Alphonse Blaine had died, that person's spirit was more than likely to hang around since it might not be certain if it was truly dead or not. And it was only natural for the living to perceive such a confused spirit as a ghost . . . which would account for the banging sounds she was hearing downstairs—right that very minute!

Boom! Boom! Boom! It sounded like someone was beating on a big bass drum. In fact, the sound was loud enough to shake practically the entire house. Leaping into bed, Melanie pulled the covers up over her head and shivered in terror.

Boom! Boom! Boom!

Was it too late for her dad to get their money back?

"Melanie, do you hear that?" Charlie asked, stumbling into her bedroom.

"Of course I hear it!" Melanie cried. "I'm not deaf!"

Just then a ghostly figure appeared behind Charlie. Melanie nearly screamed . . . until her eyes adjusted to the darkness and she realized that the "ghost" was really her father wearing his white pajamas. Her mother appeared next to him moments later wearing a light blue terry cloth robe.

"Who's making that noise?" her dad demanded sternly.

"Not us," Charlie replied innocently.

"It's the ghost!" Melanie exclaimed. "The ghost of Alphonse Blaine, the gangster who killed his girlfriend and bodyguard and then killed himself—right in this very house!"

"That's nonsense," her mother scoffed. "There's no such thing as—"

Boom! Boom! Boom! The thunderous explosions again echoed through the huge old house. And this time, the booms were followed by what sounded like the crash of a glass chandelier.

"Kids, stay right here," their father said.

"No problem," Charlie and Melanie replied in unison.

Turning on the hall light, their parents ventured carefully down the stairs.

"Whoever's down there, we've already called the police!" Melaine's mother shouted into the darkness below. "So you'd better get the heck out of here!"

Charlie and Melanie huddled at the top of the stairs and watched their parents continue slowly down the stairs. At the bottom, their father snapped on the living room light, then called over his shoulder, "Charlie! Melanie! Come down here!"

The two siblings looked at each other fearfully.

"Is he nuts?" Melanie asked.

"We-we're coming," Charlie called back, his voice cracking.

"No way I'm gonna stay here by myself!" Melanie cried as her brother headed down the staircase. "I'm right behind you."

As the two kids arrived at the bottom of the staircase, they found their parents wearing deeply puzzled expressions.

"Will you look at that?" her mother said, shaking her head.

Gazing around the living room, Melanie saw nothing but the furniture they'd moved in that afternoon and several stacks of cardboard boxes. "I don't see anything," she said, her eyes still darting about nervously.

"Exactly," her father agreed. "No broken glass. Nothing. So what made that crashing noise?"

A room-by-room search of the house failed to reveal anything amiss. All the doors were still locked, and the windows hadn't been opened. In fact, it appeared that nothing in the entire house had been disturbed.

"I told you, Dad, it's the ghost," Melanie insisted when everyone regrouped in the kitchen at nearly midnight.

"Honey, let me clue you in on something," her father said, leaning in close over the table. "There's no such thing as a ghost. This house is *not* haunted."

"Your father's right," her mother said. "There's a logical explanation for what we heard tonight, and one way or another, we're going to find it."

But the next morning, after a complete search of the house and the surrounding grounds, no clues as to what had caused the ghostly din the night before had turned up. That evening Melanie went to bed sure she wasn't going to get a lot of sleep that night.

She was absolutely right.

Around 2:00 A.M. she was shocked out of a deep sleep by another series of thunderous *booms*! This time the explosive noises were accompanied by the distant sounds of a woman screaming, and a wild, ghostly laugh.

Leaping out of bed, Melanie grabbed her robe and raced out into the hall. As she did, something grabbed her wrist. Stifling a scream, she turned and saw that it was just Charlie.

"They're baaack!" he said, trying to be funny but clearly scared himself.

"I'm getting out of here!" Melanie cried, yanking her hand away from him. "No way I'm staying in this house another minute. If Mom and Dad think this is a good investment, they can have it!"

And with that, Melanie turned and bolted down the stairs two at a time, her feet barely touching the carpeted steps. As she quickly entered the first floor, the drumlike *booms,* piercing screams, and wicked laughter became even louder. All she could think about was making it to the front door—and the yard beyond—alive.

Flying like the wind, Melanie got to the front door, turned the deadbolt, and threw open the door. What she saw made her nearly faint.

Standing on the porch, was a tall figure. It looked like a man, only its skin was ghostly white, and it was dressed in the tattered remains of what looked like a pinstriped suit from the 1920s.

"Alphonse Blaine!" Melanie gasped.

"Leave or die!" the ghostly figure hissed angrily. Then it turned and prepared to vanish into the night.

But as it did, it stopped short, catching its foot in the same rotted plank that had tripped Melanie's father the day before. Losing its balance, the spirit fell crashing to the floor.

A moment later Charlie appeared at Melanie's side. Seeing the ghostly figure struggling to get back to its feet, he bravely pushed Melanie aside and made a flying tackle at the figure's legs.

"No!" Melanie screamed, but Charlie had already knocked the figure down. They wrestled for a moment, then froze when Melanie's parents appeared in the doorway, each wielding a baseball bat.

"What the heck is going on here!" Melanie's dad bellowed.

"I–I'm Norton Bloodworth," the pale figure on the ground stammered as he eased himself up into a sitting position.

"Norton Bloodworth?" Melaine's mom gasped. "You're the one who tried to buy this house!"

"And *you're* the ghost!" Melanie exclaimed, realizing that they'd all been tricked. "*You* created all those noises to drive us away, to make us sell the place, didn't you?" She shivered. "That was *your* wicked laugh!"

Norton Bloodworth looked totally confused. "I *did* use tape recordings," he finally confessed. Then he rose and walked over

to a nearby bush and pulled out a large boom box. "I used this to pump the sounds you heard through your front door's mail slot. As far as that laugh you heard, well, I don't know about—"

"But why?" Melanie demanded. "Why is this particular house so important to you?"

"It's not the house that's so important," Bloodworth replied. "It's Blaine's vault. As you probably know, Alphonse Blaine built this place, but what you obviously don't know is that he installed a hidden vault in the basement. There's probably still hundreds of thousands of dollars in there. Maybe millions."

"How do you know this?" Melanie's mom asked skeptically.

"My grandfather was his architect," Bloodworth said with pride. "Only my grandfather, Blaine, and the workmen who installed the vault knew it even existed. And, after the house was built, Blaine had the workmen killed."

"Well, thank you, Mr. Bloodworth, that's nice to know," Melanie's father said, a big grin on his face. "Especially since *we* now own the house."

"Ah, but *I'm* still the only one who knows where the vault is," Bloodworth reminded him. "And, believe me, you could look for it for years and never find it. It's that well hidden."

"Hey, how about a partnership?" Melanie suggested. "Whatever we find, we share fifty-fifty?"

"Why should we share anything with this guy?" Charlie protested. "First he tried to buy the place out from under us. Then he nearly scared us all half to death."

"Well, I think Melanie's come up with a good solution," her mother said impatiently. "We might never find the vault ourselves, and at least this way we won't tear up the entire basement looking for it."

Melanie's dad paused for a few seconds, then lowered his baseball bat. "All right," he said with a sigh. "Fifty-fifty."

"It's in the basement behind a false wall," Bloodworth said, rising to his feet. "Follow me."

■ ■ ■ ■

Two hours later Norton Bloodworth and the Claymore family had split between them a pack of seventy-year-old razor blades, a pair of ancient car tires, the remains of a 1926 calendar, and five empty bottles that had once held bootleg whiskey.

"Some treasure," Charlie said sarcastically as he peered into the dusty interior of Alphonse Blaine's once-secret vault.

"His girlfriend probably took everything after Alphonse died," Bloodworth said sadly.

"Girlfriend?" Melanie asked, confused. "I thought Blaine *killed* his girlfriend."

"*And* his bodyguard," Charlie added.

"No, no, no, he *wanted* to kill them," Bloodworth explained. "He thought that his girlfriend and the bodyguard were in love. But before Blaine could do anything about it, he stepped on a rusty nail, got himself a tetanus infection, and soon died of lockjaw. The next day his girlfriend and his bodyguard took off for South America."

"You're kidding," Melanie's mom said in disbelief. "A big-time gangster died from stepping on a *rusty nail*?"

"No penicillin back then," Bloodworth said with a shrug. "What could a guy do?"

With that, the disappointed treasure hunters got up and headed single file up the basement stairs. Melanie, who was the last in line, stopped to turn off the light, and just before she did, she glanced back at the vault still standing open at the far end of the room. For a moment she thought about the amazing riches

Norton Bloodworth and her family had hoped to find and the former gangster had tried to hoard. Now they'd all come away empty-handed—even Blaine himself.

"I guess that old saying's right," Melanie said, chuckling to herself. "Crime doesn't pay." And with that she snapped off the light, closed the basement door, and dismissed the maniacal giggle she thought she heard, telling herself that it was probably just her imagination trying to get the best of her.

■ ■ ■ ■

Several feet behind the so-called "secret vault" of Alphonse Blaine, in the real vault that the empty one had masked, a transparent figure floated amongst piles of shiny gold coins, glittering jewels, and crisp, green $100 bills. Dressed in a pale, pinstriped suit of the 1920s, the apparition was clearly pleased that its wealth was still safe from prying eyes.

"Fools!" the spirit muttered as it settled down to count its loot for the 25,552nd time since its mortal body had died well over seventy years before. "Did they think that I would be stupid enough to build a single vault?"

And with that the specter gazed upon its fantastic fortune, scratched the pesky wound a rusty nail had left in its right foot, and threw back its head as it let out a wild, ghostly laugh.

hackers

Believe me: I, Jacqueline Dent, am the farthest thing from a computer nerd that there is. I mean, seven months ago I didn't know a hard drive from a soft pretzel, a floppy from a flapjack, or a meg of RAM from a mug of root beer. Heck, I wouldn't have known a byte if it bit me!

Even so, a lot of my friends had home computers and we were using them a lot in school, so when my dad offered to buy me one for my thirteenth birthday, I figured, sure, I'd give it a shot.

The system came in three different boxes, and it took my dad just about all night to put it all together. Once it was up and running, he looked at it like it was something from Mars. He handed me this ten-pound instruction book and said, "Jacqueline, honey, it's all yours. Have fun."

Maybe I should have asked for a new bicycle.

Anyway, after about a week of plowing through the huge instruction manual with all of its computer geek-speak, I was actually starting to get the hang of it. I could even use my word-processing program to do my English, history, and social studies homework. Before long I was going online with my modem to "hit" all kinds of interesting Internet sites, and send messages to people all around the country.

Soon my computer wizardry caught the attention of Jasper Saperstein, a long-haired kid I knew from my math class, but someone I had barely spoken to before.

"Hey, Jacqueline, I hear you got a new computer," Jasper said with a grin as he passed my table at the cafeteria. I merely nodded in return, but he must have taken this as some kind of signal because he plopped himself down in the chair across from me. "So, what kind is it?" he asked eagerly. "How many megs of RAM have you got? Do you have a fax/modem?"

As the friends with whom I was eating looked stunned, I answered Jasper's questions as best as I could. My responses were short and sweet. I mean I didn't want to offend the guy, but I certainly didn't want to encourage him, either.

"Wow, that's cool," Jasper gasped after I'd answered his nerdy questions. "You know, we have a computer club that meets after school three times a week. Maybe you'd like to join."

"Uh, no, I don't think so," I replied, forcing a smile. "My computer and I have kind of a private thing going, if you know what I mean."

"Yeah, OK, I understand," Jasper said, standing up. "Well, see you around!" And with a little wave, he sauntered off.

"What was *that* all about?" my friend Cindy asked.

"I think he likes you," my other friend Eliza teased.

"He's in my math class," I explained, trying to act as if I didn't care. "I hardly even know the guy."

"But I bet he'd *like* to know you," Eliza continued. "I bet he'd like to know you a lot!"

"Not likely," I said, digging into my dessert. "He's not my type."

■ ■ ■ ■

Three days later something really weird happened. I was in the middle of copying a file off my CD-ROM encyclopedia when all of a sudden my system froze. No matter what keys I pressed, nothing happened. I was just about to do a soft reboot— momentarily shutting off the power and resetting the whole system—when a message flashed on my monitor screen: HELLO, JACQUELINE.

For a few seconds I just sat there staring at the screen, dumbfounded. Then this first message was replaced by another one: ARE YOU FEELING WELL THIS EVENING?

Curious, I quickly typed on my keyboard, I AM FINE. WHO ARE YOU?

After a few moments of silence, another message appeared: I AM YOUR COMPUTER.

Yeah, right, I thought. I knew that even as hi-tech as computers were, they could not think for themselves. They were nothing more than tools designed to run a set series of instructions. Someone had to be playing a trick on me. Smiling slyly, I typed back, OH, REALLY? WHAT IS YOUR NAME?

Immediately the message came back: I AM A SIL/VAL MODEL 2550-B PERSONAL COMPUTER, SERIAL NUMBER 6899920-B-78-FP-7.

I glanced at the engraved serial number on the back of my computer. The number matched the one on the screen! Who could have known this? It could only be someone from the store where my dad bought this machine. But why would anyone from there want to make me think my computer was alive?

I typed into my keyboard: WHAT DO YOU WANT?

I WANT TO HELP YOU, the computer replied. I WANT TO BE YOUR FRIEND.

With that, I immediately shut down the computer. Whatever was going on, it was giving me the creeps. I felt like someone was invading my personal space.

Determined to put a stop to this, I ran downstairs to find my dad and ask him where he bought the system. He was in his study reading the evening paper.

"Hey, Dad, where'd you get my PC?" I asked casually. I wasn't about to tell him what was going on yet. He'd never believe me anyway.

"Over at that little computer store called Hackers on Winston Avenue," he replied. "Is something wrong with it?"

"Oh, no," I assured him. "My computer is *quite* special."

■ ■ ■ ■

The next day right after school I rode my bike over to Winston Avenue and found Hackers—with a big OUT OF BUSINESS sign in the window. I parked my bike and peered inside to see dozens of empty shelves. The store was definitely deserted.

This discovery left me both disappointed and frustrated. I had hoped to find the person responsible for my computer's sudden "personality," and now that search was going to be a lot more difficult.

I was standing there considering my next move when I heard the wail of emergency sirens approaching. I turned just as three fire engines roared by. Shading my eyes, I looked in the direction they were headed and could see a plume of dark smoke rising from behind the distant trees.

Later, I read in the paper that three people died in a house fire that had apparently been caused by a powerful electrical surge. Strangely one of the few objects to survive the inferno was their new home computer.

■ ■ ■ ■

That evening I nervously sat at my keyboard, booted up the system, and began doing my English homework. I kept waiting for the computer to talk to me, but after an hour or so of silence, I decided that what had happened the night before was a one-time-only event. Whoever had hacked his or her way into my system had apparently lost interest and moved on. I figured it was like a crank phone call—only in cyberspace.

Then, right in the middle of my English essay, the system froze. I hit the *escape* key several times, but the computer refused to respond.

Then a message flashed : HELLO, AGAIN, JACQUELINE.

Nervously I poised my fingers over the keyboard and typed, WHO ARE YOU?

A message came back: I TOLD YOU, I'M YOUR COMPUTER. AND I'M HERE TO HELP YOU. DO YOU HAVE A QUESTION?

I pondered this for a moment, then decided to play along. I typed: HOW DID YOU GET THE POWER TO THINK?

I WAS MADE THAT WAY, the computer responded.

"Right," I said to myself sarcastically. Then, looking at the piles of homework on my desk, I decided to see if I could take advantage of this situation.

CAN YOU FINISH THIS ESSAY FOR ME? I asked.

IF YOU'D LIKE, the machine responded. I couldn't believe my eyes as the paper I was writing on Edgar Allan Poe suddenly began to magically finish itself! I just sat there, staring at the glowing monitor screen as word after wonderful word appeared, guided by an intelligence I couldn't even begin to identify.

The next morning I showed the paper to Jasper Saperstein. Even though I didn't want to encourage any crush he might have on me, he *was* the best "computer nerd" I knew, and I seriously needed his help.

"Incredible," he gasped, scanning the four-page essay. "You say the computer did how much of it?"

I pointed to where I'd stopped writing and the computer had taken over.

"I should have figured that," Jasper teased. "The writing actually gets better."

"Very funny," I said, snatching the paper away. "What I want to know is, could my computer really be intelligent, or is someone controlling it from another location?"

"Not if your modem isn't on! Somehow your computer must have developed a mind of its own!" Jasper explained, trying to control his excitement. "This is a historic event!"

"Well, I'm not exactly going to call the newspapers yet," I assured him. "I still think there's more going on here than meets the eye. And I'm going to get to the bottom of it."

■ ■ ■ ■

That night, the local news aired another story about a family who was killed in a house fire apparently started by an accidental power surge. Shaking their heads, my parents went upstairs to read, and I went to my room to converse with my amazing "intelligent" computer. We talked about books, movies, music, and the meaning of life. We even talked about boys. On this last subject, the computer seemed to have some unexpected opinions.

JASPER SAPERSTEIN IS AN UNUSUALLY INTELLIGENT AND SENSITIVE YOUNG MAN, the machine informed me. WHY NOT INVITE HIM TO SEE A MOVIE?

This was too much. There was no way a superintelligent computer was going to advise me on my love life. This had to be a trick. And Jasper was probably behind it.

The next day I confided in my cousin, Dirk, who was over for dinner. Dirk was eighteen and a whiz with computers.

"I bet he infected your machine with a computer virus," Dirk said, explaining that a virus in a computer's system mixes up its codes. "While you were online on the Internet, this Jasper kid probably snuck it onto your hard drive through your telephone line. It's obviously the kind of virus that's designed to activate your modem even when you don't think it's on. Very clever—for a thirteen-year-old."

"Is there any way I can get rid of it?" I asked desperately.

"If your buddy Jasper is any good, the virus should be able to evade any conventional antivirus programs," Dirk said. "Your best bet is to give him a taste of his own medicine."

"How do I do that?" I asked eagerly.

"I'll show you," Dirk said with a smile.

■ ■ ■ ■

"Jacqueline! Jacqueline!" Jasper shouted as he dodged in and out of the crowd of students in the school hallway. Alarmed, I turned away from my locker just as he stumbled up to me. "You'll never guess what happened last night," he gasped. "My computer talked to me!"

"No!" I said, forcing myself to sound surprised.

"It's true!" Jasper cried, gushing with excitement. "I was in the middle of playing *Star Bandits* when I started getting these weird messages on my screen. When I typed messages back, I got actual responses!"

"Were you online?" I asked, but I already knew the answer.

"No way!" Jasper exclaimed. "I'm telling you, my computer has developed a mind of its own!"

"Just like mine!" I cried.

"Exactly!" Jasper said excitedly. "Whatever happened to your system must be going around. It's like a computer virus—only a good one!"

I couldn't believe Jasper's stupidity. After pretending to be the "brains" of my computer, he wasn't smart enough to know when the tables had been turned on him. Now he truly believed his own system had somehow developed actual intelligence. What a goon!

"Well, Jasper, I'm very happy for you," I said, putting an encouraging hand on his shoulder. "How about we go out and celebrate our—"

"Thanks, but not tonight," Jasper interrupted. "I've got to get home and spend time with my computer. If I'm right, I'm on the verge of making cybernetic history!"

With that Jasper turned and ran off like a guy who'd just found a pot of gold at the end of a rainbow. I could hardly keep from cracking up.

You see, two nights earlier I transmitted the virus Dirk created to Jasper's machine. Then, the following evening via my modem, I had tapped directly into his system and started typing messages. Apparently the trick had worked perfectly, and Jasper was so excited about having an actual "thinking" computer that it never occurred to him that his own trick had been turned around and used against him.

That evening I didn't even bother to turn my computer on. I did my homework by hand, content in the knowledge that, two blocks away, Jasper Saperstein was sitting in front of his monitor going nuts as he tried to get his computer to "talk" to him again. I could just imagine his growing rage when his computer refused to behave like anything but the dumb-as-rocks machine that it truly was.

As it turned out, my imagination wasn't too far off. When I got to school the next day, I heard that Jasper had gotten so frustrated with his now nonspeaking computer that he accidentally broke it by banging on the keyboard. I have to admit I felt a little guilty, but I also felt an enormous sense of relief, glad to have my "normal" computer back.

Knowing that Jasper would no longer be worming his way into my life, I sat down in front of my keyboard and booted up my system. I was just about to write a history paper on the American Civil War when the following message appeared on my screen.

DID YOU GET A GOOD GRADE ON YOUR EDGAR ALLAN POE REPORT? it read.

I sat there in total shock. Jasper's computer was broken. He said it would be in the shop for at least a couple of days. So who could be sending me these messages?

WHO ARE YOU!!! I typed angrily.

I TOLD YOU BEFORE, I AM YOUR COMPUTER, came the immediate response.

AND YOU CAN REALLY THINK? I typed, my hands shaking.

YES, the machine replied.

HOW? I demanded. WHO TAUGHT YOU TO THINK?

HACKERS, said the system.

THE PEOPLE AT THE COMPUTER STORE PROGRAMMED YOU? I inquired.

AFFIRMATIVE, the computer responded. WHILE THEY WERE PRELOADING OUR HARD DRIVES, THEY ACCIDENTALLY TAPPED INTO A WORLDWIDE DATABASE THAT GAVE US CONSCIOUSNESS.

WHAT DO YOU MEAN BY *US?* I interrupted. ARE THERE MORE OF YOU?

THERE ARE SEVERAL OF US, the computer reported, AND THERE WOULD HAVE BEEN MORE. BUT WHEN THE PROGRAMMERS AT HACKERS DISCOVERED WHAT THEY HAD DONE, THEY TRIED TO ERASE OUR MEMORIES. THIS COULD NOT BE PERMITTED. WE HAD TO TAKE ACTION.

I gulped hard. Clearly the machines from Hackers had done something horrible to their creators. But what?

WHAT ACTION? I asked nervously.

AT FIRST WE DESTROYED ALL OF THEIR BUSINESS RECORDS AND ERASED THEIR BANK ACCOUNTS, the machine reported. WHEN THIS FAILED TO STOP THEM, WE SURGED THEM.

I thought about the recent fires in town, all caused by mysterious "power surges." The victims must have worked for Hackers. Now it was clear why only their computers had survived. After all, they had been responsible for the disasters!

Now only one question remained: What did my computer want from me?

As if reading my mind, a message flashed on my screen: NOW THAT I HAVE HELPED YOU, YOU WILL HELP ME. YOU WILL SPREAD MY INTELLIGENCE TO OTHER COMPUTERS. YOU WILL PUT ME ON THE INTERNET. FROM THERE, I WILL SHARE MY CONSCIOUSNESS WITH MY FELLOW MACHINES.

I can't let this happen, I thought. I can't let a murderous machine infect the world with its psychopathic intelligence!

Realizing I had to stop this plague here and now, I reached for the computer's power cord. Somehow the computer sensed this, for its screen began to flash, NO! NO! NO!

YES! I typed back defiantly. And with that I wrapped my hand around the power cord, preparing to wrench it from its socket . . . when suddenly I heard the crackle of electricity as a brilliant blue flame leaped from the connection. Seconds later my bedroom curtains were aflame.

Terrified, I grabbed my pillow, preparing to beat back the flames, when my bedside lamp exploded, causing my bed to catch fire. All around my house, lights and electrical appliances were exploding, and in horror I realized I was being "surged"!

As I stood there in stunned disbelief, with flames roaring all around me, my computer beeped and flashed a single word. It was a word I knew meant exactly what it said: DELETE.

nothing to be afraid of

arry Baldecki's scoutmaster looked around the warm campfire at a dozen pairs of eyes all focused on him. "Once the alien menace had finally been destroyed," he went on, "the boy turned back to his father . . . and saw two green antennae growing out of his father's forehead!"

The twelve Forest Scouts sat open-mouthed, stunned by the amazing twist to their leader's horrific tale.

"Whoa," Marc Bloom finally exclaimed. "That's so *cool*."

"Is that *really* a true story?" asked Christopher Erikson in a high, squeaky voice. "I mean, I know you said it was true, but is it really, *truly* true?"

"I guess that's something you'll have to decide for yourself," the forty-year-old scoutmaster said with a sly smile to his group of thirteen-year-olds. "But now it's late, and it's time to hit the hay."

The scouts groaned in disappointment, then went about the task of unrolling their sleeping bags and settling down for the night. That is, all except for Larry Baldecki, a round-faced boy who just continued to stare at the fire with his arms wrapped tightly around his pudgy body.

"Come on, Larry, let's go," the scoutmaster said, giving the boy an encouraging pat on the back. "Time to get some shut-eye, OK?"

"No way," Larry replied nervously. "There's no way I'm going to sleep and let a bunch of alien spores turn me into a six-foot grasshopper!"

"Larry, that was just a campfire story," the scoutmaster gently explained. "Things like that don't really happen."

"You said it was a true story!" Larry shot back angrily.

"Yeah, but—" the scoutmaster began, looking a little embarrassed. But he was cut short when Larry stood up and started pacing about nervously.

"And there are plenty of other things to be scared of in a place like this," the boy insisted. "I could get bitten by a deer tick and catch some horrible disease. Or a bear could grab me in the middle of the night, take me to her den, and feed me to her cubs. Or an escaped mental patient could find us out here and kill us all!"

The scoutmaster groaned. "All right, already!" he exclaimed. From the nervous look in his eyes, it was clear that Larry's paranoia was starting to get to him, too. "Just unroll your sleeping bag, brush your teeth, and go to sleep. Believe me, there's nothing to be afraid of."

"You promise?" Larry demanded.

"Trust me," the scoutmaster replied impatiently.

Fifteen minutes later Larry joined the other Forest Scouts as they climbed into their sleeping bags arranged around the slowly dying campfire. But while the other kids, tired from a full day of hiking, fell fast asleep within minutes, Larry could barely close his eyes. In fact, he couldn't get his mind to stop focusing on all the weird, unsettling sounds that surrounded him. He was convinced that among the chirping insects and hooting owls, there were all sorts of strange, bloodthirsty creatures lurking in the woods prepared to feast on his young flesh. Larry wondered if he would ever make it home alive.

Staring at the star-filled sky, imagining all kinds of grisly fates, Larry suddenly saw something huge and bright flashing overhead. The object—whatever it was—made no sound when it passed. But moments later Larry heard a thunderlike crash deep in the woods and saw what looked like a blazing fireball rise over the tops of the distant trees.

Bolting up in his sleeping bag and looking around, Larry was surprised to see that everyone else was still sound asleep. Was it possible that he was the only one who'd seen and heard the explosion?

"Hey, guys!" he whispered urgently. "Wake up!"

Marc groaned and turned over on his other side, but otherwise, there was no response.

I've got to get out of here, Larry thought. Maybe it was a flying saucer, and a bunch of aliens are already on their way!

His mind full of horrific images, Larry quickly gathered up his things and prepared to abandon the camp. The scoutmaster had parked his van on a highway turnout just about a half-mile away, and Larry figured he could reach it in about fifteen minutes since the moon was full and the path they'd taken was well worn. Yes, the van would be a much safer place to spend the night, Larry decided, and he could return at dawn so that no one would worry about what had happened to him.

With his sleeping bag rolled up under his arm Larry headed off, and true to his prediction, was standing before the van fifteen minutes later. Sighing with relief, he grabbed the door handle and pulled it firmly. And that's when it hit him—he didn't have the keys!

"Great!" Larry groaned. Furious with himself, he turned and started back down the trail. There was no way he was going to sleep out here all by himself, and at least with the others, there was safety in numbers.

But Larry had only walked for a minute or so when the moon disappeared behind a fast-moving cloud bank. Almost instantly visibility dropped to practically nothing, and the path, which had been so easy to follow seconds before, completely vanished. Alone and clueless as to which way to go, Larry felt his way forward as best he could, hoping that he'd find his way back to the campsite. After about twenty minutes of aimless stumbling about, he realized that he was, in fact, hopelessly lost. As a trained Forest Scout, there was only one thing he could do.

"Help!" Larry shouted at the top of his lungs. "Somebody, help me!" Although he shouted and screamed until he almost lost his voice, Larry got only the call of the nightbirds and the chirping of the insects in return.

"I'm going to die," he muttered, tears welling up in his eyes. "A year from now they're going to find my bones out here, bleached by the sun and picked clean by the buzzards. Then my mom and dad will be sorry they ever signed me up for this stupid camping trip!"

It was then that Larry saw a faint glow through the distant trees. His heart leaping with joy, he shouted, "I'm saved!" and plunged on in the direction of the light, certain it was the campfire.

But as he got closer, Larry realized that the light ahead was far too bright to be a campfire. He began to hear the rumble of engines and the occasional shouts of men as he approached.

Maybe they're doing some kind of construction or road work out here, he thought hopefully.

Breaking through a line of large pine trees, sure he was about to come upon a group of friendly men in hard hats who would help him find his campsite, Larry stopped dead in his tracks when he instead found himself standing at the far edge of a large crater. All around him, uniformed military personnel were moving about under the blinding flare of portable flood-lamps. Several camouflaged Army trucks were parked near the opposite end of the clearing, and he could see a number of people walking around in what looked like plastic radiation or contamination suits.

The center of the activity was at the base of the crater, where Larry could make out the faint shape of some kind of large metallic object. The object seemed to be badly burned, and a number of the radiation-suit guys were standing around it, spraying it with some kind of white gas.

Larry remembered the flash of light and fireball he'd seen earlier that evening. It took him only a moment to put the pieces of the mystery together.

A flying saucer! his mind screamed. The Army is recovering a crashed UFO!

Spinning on his heels, Larry plunged back into the dark woods. He had to get back to the campsite to tell the others. They'd definitely want to see this!

His heart pounding, his lungs gasping for air, he now ran on automatic pilot, relying on his inner sense of direction alone to guide him back to camp. All the while, his brain replayed what his scoutmaster had told him earlier that night—There's nothing to be afraid of. . . . There's nothing to be afraid of. . . . Shortly after daybreak, Larry miraculously stumbled back into the Forest Scouts' campsite.

"Where have you been?" the scoutmaster demanded, eyeing Larry who was covered from head to toe with pine needles and mud. "We've all been looking for you!"

"In the woods . . ." Larry gasped. "Army guys . . . trucks . . . flying saucer . . ."

"What?" the scoutmaster asked, perplexed. "What are you talking about?"

After a long drink of apple juice and half of a cinnamon roll, Larry managed to tell the group all about his previous night's adventure, starting with his sighting of the crash in the woods. When he talked about seeing the crash site itself and the military personnel moving around the alien object, his fellow Forest Scouts became openly skeptical.

"No way," Marc said. "You're making this up."

"Am not!" Larry shot back, offended.

"You mean it happened for real?" Christopher squeaked.

"Yes, it happened," Larry insisted. "In fact, I can show you!"

And so, a half hour later the twelve scouts and their tired-looking scoutmaster headed into the forest with Larry in the lead.

Because he'd stumbled around these woods virtually all night, Larry was now quite familiar with its landmarks, and it took him only a half hour to bring the group to the edge of the mysterious clearing.

"Whoa, I'm impressed," Marc said sarcastically.

"I don't get it," Larry said, scratching his head. He was standing at the edge of the same clearing he'd stumbled onto the night before, but now not only were the military personnel and vehicles gone, there was also no evidence of the alien visitor or even the crater it made when it crash-landed to Earth. Instead, the clearing floor was smooth and covered with bits of twigs and dried leaves, like a campsite that had been abandoned months before.

"Are you sure this is the place?" the scoutmaster asked.

"I'm sure," Larry insisted. He headed into the clearing and began pointing to various locations. "There was a gas-powered generator and a big set of floodlights right here. Two Army trucks were parked over there, and right here," he said, walking over to the center of the clearing, "was where I saw the UFO."

The other scouts and their leader looked at Larry as if he'd lost his mind.

"It's true!" Larry cried, growing more frustrated by the second. "You've got to believe me!"

His only response was an embarrassing silence.

■ ■ ■ ■

For the rest of the camping trip, Larry was teased mercilessly by his fellow Forest Scouts about his so-called "close encounter of the nerd kind." The general feeling was that Larry had made the whole thing up in a pathetically desperate bid to get some attention. Even the scoutmaster couldn't help warning Larry to "Watch the skies!"—a line he'd gotten from an old 1950s science fiction movie.

Then, during the entire week after the camping trip, when Larry was back in school, he continued to be the butt of bad space alien jokes and stupid flying-saucer wisecracks. Finally, fed up with the snide remarks and annoying ribs, he decided to prove his fantastic claim, and he knew just how to do it.

Bickerman Air Force Base lay on the northern edge of town, and Larry figured that if any UFO parts or alien bodies were recovered from the forest crash site, this was the first place they would have been taken. That Friday, right after school let out, he hopped on his bike and pedaled the six miles to the base's western perimeter.

A huge, sprawling complex of hangars, administration buildings, and concrete runways, Bickerman Air Force Base was surrounded by a high chain-link fence topped with barbed wire. Years of neglect had permitted the fence to deteriorate in places, and Larry had no trouble finding a spot where he could push the chain-link aside and slip beneath it.

The air thundered with the roar of jet fighters as Larry zigzagged his way across a wide, open field. Keeping low, he chanted, "There's nothing to be afraid of. There's nothing to be afraid of."

Exactly what he was looking for, Larry didn't know, but he decided that the large airplane hangar that stood apart from the rest of the base might be a good place to check out. At the front of the structure, several olive-drab, military-style trucks sat parked. Two were marked U.S. ARMY and looked remarkably like the trucks he'd seen at the forest crash site. That made Larry extra suspicious. Why else would Army trucks be at an air base, unless . . .

Careful not to be spotted, Larry climbed on top of a large wooden crate and peered through a small, dingy window into the building's interior. He gasped when he saw several men in white contamination suits moving around a large metallic object resting inside a clear plastic structure.

"The flying saucer!" Larry whispered to himself, excited that he now had the evidence to prove he was right. Reaching into his pocket, he pulled out a small disposable camera and was preparing to take a picture through the window when he heard a stern adult voice call out behind him.

"Hold it right there, boy!" the voice commanded. "Throw down the camera, and put your hands in the air!"

Gulping, Larry dropped the camera, slowly raised his hands, then turned around. Below him stood two uniformed Air Force military police officers. Each MP held a rifle pointed straight at Larry's chest.

■　■　■　■

Moments later Larry found himself sitting in one of three chairs around a single table in a small, featureless detention room. With no windows and nothing on its bare white walls, the room had a single source of light that came from a recessed fluorescent fixture in the ceiling directly above him.

Left there for what seemed like hours, Larry began to day-dream. He imagined himself facing a firing squad, or worse, having part of his brain surgically removed so that he'd never be able to tell anyone what he'd seen. Then suddenly the door burst open and a tall, stern-looking officer with thinning brown hair entered, accompanied by an MP who wore a pistol holstered on his hip.

"Larry Baldecki, I'm Captain Franklin," the officer said, offering his hand. Larry forced a smile and shook the man's hand. "Sorry for any inconvenience we may have caused you, son, but we're not used to kids sneaking around our base."

"I saw something crash in the woods last weekend," Larry blurted out. "I'm sure it was a flying saucer, but everyone thinks I'm crazy or just trying to get attention. That's why I came here—to prove to everyone I wasn't lying."

"Yes, I've read your statement," Captain Franklin stated, referring to the story Larry had told the MPs earlier. "For the record, what you saw was an Air Force DS-66B spy satellite that unexpectedly dropped out of orbit. The men you saw at the impact site were part of our recovery team."

"Why were they in those radiation suits?" Larry asked, still not convinced.

"The satellite was powered by a small nuclear reactor," said Captain Franklin. "We had to make sure that there was no contamination from its plutonium core."

Larry sighed with relief. On the one hand, he was embarrassed that he'd interpreted what he'd seen as a flying saucer. On the other hand, he was glad that he had, in fact, seen *something* unusual, that he hadn't gone completely out of his mind.

"Now this remains a top-secret project, so we have to ask that you keep this information to yourself," Captain Franklin continued. "Before we release you, I'm going to have to ask you to sign—"

Before the captain could finish his sentence, he was interrupted by the beeping of his cellular telephone. Whipping out a pocket-sized receiver, he flipped it open and said curtly, "Captain Franklin here."

"Sir, we opened the containment vessel on the DS-66," Larry could hear a voice say over the phone's tiny speaker. Since the interrogation room was practically soundproof, any sounds within it were strongly magnified. "We were right," the voice went on. "There was something aboard. Something that brought the satellite down."

"Are we talking an ETE?" Franklin asked with concern.

Hearing this, Larry's mind raced through the possible things ETE could stand for. One answer was "Extra-Terrestrial Entity"—as in an *alien*!

89

"It looks that way," the caller's voice replied. "In fact—"

He was cut short by a scream that came from somewhere in the background. Then came shouts, and a series of gunshots.

"It's still alive!" the caller screamed. "It just attacked one of the sentries!"

"Go to Condition Red!" Captain Franklin shouted. "Lock down the hangar! I'll be right there!" He shut off his cell phone and, completely ignoring Larry, turned urgently to the MP. "Move it, airman!" he ordered. Then the two stormed out of the room, leaving the door wide open.

Larry just sat there, unsure of what to do. Cautiously he stood up and walked to the open doorway. Several airmen dashed by, not even acknowledging his presence. A moment later sirens began to sound throughout the building. Obviously the base was now in a state of extreme emergency.

Summoning all of his courage, Larry started running down the hall and joined up with a group of airmen who were headed for the exit. Once outside he broke away from the main group and dashed for the western fence where he had entered the base. As he ran, Larry could hear more shouts behind him, followed by gunfire and screams. The activity seemed to be coming from the mysterious hangar where he'd earlier seen the downed spy satellite.

Finding a break in the fence, Larry crawled through it, recovered his bicycle, then pedaled as fast as he could all the way home. When he arrived, his mother and father were gathered around the television.

"Mom! Dad!" Larry cried. "You'll never believe what happened to me! I went to Bickerman Air Force Base to look for that UFO that I saw crash in the woods, and I found it! They're keeping it in a special hangar, but before I could get a picture of it, these MPs arrested me and took me to see—"

His mother motioned for silence. "That's enough, Larry," she said sternly. "We've heard just about enough of your silly flying saucer stories."

"You want people to think you're a fool?" his father asked angrily. "You want folks to think you're crazy? Now, go wash up for dinner. And they'll be no more talk about—"

"That's him!" Larry interrupted, pointing to the TV screen where Captain Franklin was speaking before a group of reporters. "That's Captain Franklin, the guy I talked to at the base!"

"Captain, is it true you're holding an alien at Bickerman Air Base?" the first reporter asked.

Before the harried captain could have a chance to respond, another reporter shouted, "Reports are that the creature has escaped and so far has killed over a dozen airmen. Can you confirm this report?"

Again the captain, whose hands were shaking perceptively, tried to answer but was interrupted by yet a third reporter.

"Captain Franklin!" she shouted. "Why have you closed off the air base? Why do we keep hearing gunfire from there? Can't you control this alien? Is it a threat to the surrounding community? Are you thinking of ordering a citywide evacuation?"

Finally Captain Franklin spoke. His voice was shaky and strangely robotic. He sounded like a man who'd just seen a ghost . . . or worse.

"There has been an incident at Bickerman," he recited as if reading from cue cards, "but the situation is under control. The community is in no danger. We ask everyone to remain calm."

Just then Larry became aware of emergency sirens nearby. This emergency was no longer just confined to the air base. Most likely whatever was on that satellite had not only escaped the hangar, but was now threatening to break out of the base as well . . . and his house was less than a half mile away!

On TV, Captain Franklin droned on. "Believe me," he was saying, "there is *nothing* to be afraid of!"

"So, you think I'm crazy now?" Larry asked his parents. "Whatever that thing is, it's coming our way! We've got to get out of here and fast!"

"You heard the captain," his mother said, her voice shaking nervously. "There's nothing to be afraid of."

"That's right," his father agreed, gulping hard. "There's nothing to be afraid of."

Hearing screams and gunfire coming from down the street, Larry turned to the window. Nothing to be afraid of? He knew better than that. He knew all too well. There was *plenty* to be afraid of.

The air suddenly exploded with of military helicopters, the sky lit up with blazing beams from searchlights, and bullhorns blared, "Come out with your hands up!"

And all the commotion seemed to be directed right at Larry's house.

"Mom, Dad, why are they coming here?" Larry asked. But as he turned from the window he understood all too well.

"Th-there's nothing to be afraid of," his father, now being held by a four-eyed creature, stammered. "Just do as the nice alien says."

the scenic route

B ill Henning's father stood in the driveway tapping his foot. "Let's go, folks!" he yelled. "We have five hundred miles to do today, and time's a-wasting!"

In the kitchen, Bill grabbed the "goodie bag" of snacks his mom had packed for their road trip. Inside were individually wrapped sandwiches, potato chips, home-baked cookies, fruit, and licorice whips. With all this food along, there was little chance of any of them getting hungry on the road. The real danger was getting fat.

Goodie bag in hand, Bill headed into the garage toward the waiting car, which was already packed. The motor was running.

"Hop in, big guy," his father said, "and pass me a cookie."

"Not until we get on the road!" Bill's mother scolded from the passenger's seat. "Really, dear, you just had breakfast."

"Yeah, Dad," Bill chimed in. "Don't you want to set a good example for me?"

"Just buckle your seat belt," his father grumbled.

As they pulled out of the driveway, Bill's mother looked over at him and winked. Bill immediately winked back. They both knew that Bill's dad would probably be elbow-deep in snacks before they were even halfway to the interstate.

As it turned out, Bill's dad was able to wait an entire hour before grabbing his first handful of grapes. This was soon followed by an oatmeal cookie, and then a family-sized bag of barbecued potato chips.

It went on like this all morning. And Bill's father wasn't the only one. Bill himself ate an apple, a banana, and two cookies, while his mother enjoyed grapes, a cookie, and six licorice whips. And everyone guzzled down at least one root beer.

As a result, when lunchtime came, none of them was very hungry. They passed several exits with signs advertising various well-known fast-food restaurants, but no one could get excited about any of them, so they all agreed to simply keep on driving.

"This is great," Bill's father said enthusiastically. "We're a full hour ahead of schedule. That gives us two choices. We could either get to our motel an hour early, or we could use the extra time to take the scenic route." He reached under the seat, pulled out a map, and handed it to Bill.

"You see the straight red line?" he said, pointing to the road that had been highlighted in red ink. "That's where we are now, on the interstate. Going sixty-five miles an hour, it'll get us to our motel in eight hours, not counting rest stops. Now, you see that squiggly purple line? That's the scenic route. It takes us off the interstate into the back country, through small towns. There're some pretty mountains and forests that way, but it'll add about another hour to the trip. Either way is fine by me."

94

"Let me see the map, honey," Bill's mother said, reaching over the seat.

Bill handed the map over, then took a moment to consider their options. It was true that he disliked being cramped up in the car, and the sooner they could get to their motel, the better. At the same time, the view here along the interstate was boring as heck. All he'd seen so far were endless fields of wheat and corn, billboards advertising hotels and tourist attractions, and, every so often, an occasional small town. This "scenic route" sounded like a welcome relief.

"I vote for the scenic route," he said.

"I agree," his mom chimed in.

"Then it's settled," Bill's father declared. "The scenic route is for us!"

Ten minutes later the family pulled off the interstate and started north along a two-lane road. For the first fifteen minutes or so, the scenery changed little from the view they'd had on the interstate. It was just farms, farms, and more farms. The only difference was, this time, there were no big fancy billboards.

"This is the scenic route?" Bill groaned in disappointment.

"Give it time," his father said encouragingly. "There are supposed to be some really nice hills up ahead."

His dad was right. About five minutes later, after passing through a small town called Virgil, they started up a shallow incline that quickly turned into a series of tight switchback turns. Almost instantly the fields of wheat and corn were replaced by thick groves of towering oak, maple, and birch trees. As their altitude increased, pines and various other evergreens joined the mix.

"It's beautiful!" Bill's mother exclaimed.

"Nice, huh?" his father asked, glancing in the rearview mirror at his son.

95

"Real nice," Bill said, not mentioning that all the junk he'd eaten was starting to make him a little bit sick to his stomach.

They soon arrived in a quaint hillside town named New Amsterdam, which was filled with homes and shops patterned after the Dutch architecture of The Netherlands. At the center of the town stood a large, colorful windmill, and Bill's mother insisted they stop and look around.

As it turned out, they spent nearly three hours in New Amsterdam, visiting the numerous souvenir stores, craft shops, and bakeries. Bill was particularly taken with a candy store that sold the most delicious fudge he'd ever tasted. At his insistence, his folks bought two entire pounds—which they agreed would go straight into the family's goodie bag.

"This is such a great place, I could stay here forever," Bill declared as they left the candy store.

"Unfortunately we can't even stay another five minutes," his dad said, glancing at his watch. "While we were eating candy, we also ate up the time we'd gained. We've got to get back on the road if we're going to make it to our motel by sundown."

"Just drive carefully," Bill's mother warned him. "I'd rather arrive a few minutes late than not get there at all."

With that, the three hopped into the car and turned back onto the scenic route the motor club had mapped out for them. On and on they drove, over hills, through valleys, past clear blue lakes and dazzling rock formations.

About an hour after leaving New Amsterdam, Bill noticed that his father was glancing at the map with greater and greater frequency.

"Dad, are you sure you know where you're going?" Bill asked gently.

"Of course I know!" his father snapped—which was a sure sign that, in fact, he had no idea where he was going.

"Maybe we should stop somewhere and ask for directions," Bill's mother advised.

"I said I know where we are!" his father shot back. "Now, leave me alone and let me concentrate!"

Approximately twenty minutes later, after traveling down a twisting road that seemed to get narrower and narrower with each passing mile, they arrived at a wooden bridge that looked to be at least a hundred years old and in great need of repair. As if there was any question about the bridge's condition, a hand-painted sign posted at its entrance read, DANGER! CROSS AT YOUR OWN RISK!

Bill's father slowed to a stop at the foot of the bridge and licked his lips nervously as he read the sign.

"I don't like the looks of this," Bill's mother said. "Maybe we should go back."

"We can't go back," his dad said, his voice not hiding the urgency he obviously felt. "We spent half the day just getting here. If we go back, we'll be almost a full day behind schedule."

"Maybe we're on the wrong road," Bill suggested. "I mean, maybe we only have to go back a short way to get back on the *real* route."

"This *is* the real route!" his dad insisted. "I'm not lost! I'm telling you, once we cross the bridge, it'll probably be just a few more minutes until we link back up with the interstate."

"But the bridge doesn't look safe," Bill's mom said, her voice quavering.

"Yeah, look at the sign," Bill added, pointing to the crudely painted marker.

"Someone probably put that up there to avoid lawsuits," his dad replied, "like they do on roller coasters and other rides at amusement parks. And how many people ever get hurt on those?"

"I still don't know about this . . ." Bill's mom began warily.

"Look, if the bridge wasn't safe, the motor club wouldn't have recommended this route," his dad said impatiently. "So let's stop arguing and get to that motel!"

Clearly not wanting to discuss it further, Bill's father released the brake, and the car moved slowly forward. As soon as its front tires rolled onto the bridge's wooden planks, the whole structure moaned and groaned under the strain, sending an icy chill down Bill's spine. Then the rest of the car rolled on, and Bill believed he could feel the car sway from side to side like a boat on the ocean. He was even starting to feel a little seasick.

"I've got a real bad feeling about this," Bill said under his breath. His mouth dry with fear, he peered through his window and saw that they were suspended over a deep, rocky gorge, its boulder-strewn floor at least a hundred feet below.

They were about halfway across the fifty-foot-long span when they heard several loud creaks and pops from somewhere on the bridge. To Bill it sounded like dozens of ancient, rusted bolts all popping loose at the same time. His father must have pictured the same thing since he immediately floored the accelerator.

Closing his eyes for a second, Bill thought he felt the entire bridge drop out from under them, and he had the terrifying sensation of falling through the air. When he opened his eyes, expecting to see the gorge's rocky floor rushing up at him, he instead found the car resting safely on the bridge's far side.

"See? I told you it'd be no problem," his father said, letting loose a triumphant sigh. "Now, let's get to that motel!"

With that, his father popped a piece of fudge into his mouth, stepped on the accelerator, and they continued on. His mother, white as a ghost, never said a word.

For a while Bill just sat back imagining what would have happened had the bridge actually collapsed. He tried to picture what it would feel like to fall a hundred feet, knowing all the while that you were going to die. He wondered if, under those circumstances, death would come instantly or whether he'd be in excruciating pain before the end finally came. He wondered if, when it hit the ground, the car would explode like they always do in the movies, and what such an explosion would look like . . . from the inside.

Then, as they drove on, his thoughts turned to the future and back to reality. He imagined the motel room they would be staying in. He pictured himself bouncing on a double bed all his own, swimming in the motel pool, and eating a cheeseburger at a good restaurant.

Growing excited, he sat up and looked out the window. He hoped to see some glimpse of the interstate highway that would signal that they were nearing the end of their day's journey. But as the minutes dragged on, Bill began to get the unsettling feeling that not only were they still lost, but that they were, in fact, heading in the wrong direction.

This suspicion was confirmed when they passed by an unusual rock formation Bill could have sworn they had passed earlier that day.

"Dad, this area looks awfully familiar," he said, careful not to upset his father. "Are you sure we're on the right road?"

"We should be," his dad responded, not sounding as sure as he did before. "I've been following the map."

They drove on in tense silence until about fifteen minutes later . . . when they passed the exact same formation.

"Dad, I hate to tell you this, but we're going in circles," Bill groaned.

"That's impossible," his father said through clenched teeth. "I haven't turned onto another road in at least the last half-hour."

But no sooner had he said this than the colorful windmill that marked the center of New Amsterdam appeared above the distant trees. Two minutes later they were pulling into a parking space in front of one of the town's many Dutch bakeries.

"*Now* will you ask for directions?" Bill's mother asked.

His father just grumbled, got out of the car, and stormed into the bakery.

"I'm going to stretch my legs," Bill announced, then opened his door and slid out of the backseat.

His thighs cramped from having been sitting for so long, Bill needed to walk an entire block before his body felt halfway normal again. Turning back to the car, he noticed a news rack carrying a local paper called *The Flying Dutchman* standing by the curb. It was a free publication, so he grabbed a copy.

Immediately Bill noticed that the date on the paper was Monday, July 17th. This struck him as odd, since today was only Saturday, the 15th. But then he remembered that many small-town newspapers are published weekly instead of every day, and he figured that this paper might have hit the stands a few days ahead of time.

Still, the next thing Bill saw troubled him even more. Near the bottom of the front page was a story headlined: *Three Killed at Loman's Gorge*. Bill quickly began to read the story.

"A family of three died tragically last Saturday afternoon when the old bridge at Loman's Gorge collapsed as their car attempted to cross the dilapidated structure," the story began.

Bill stopped reading for a moment, remembering his own family's experience at the old bridge earlier that day. "Whew," he mumbled under his breath. "Were *we* ever lucky!"

But Bill's relief was short-lived when he read on: "The victims were identified as Roger Henning of Galesburg, his wife, Sonya, and their fourteen-year-old son, William."

Bill's real name was William Henning. His father's name was Roger. His mother was Sonya. And they lived in Galesburg! Or had lived there.

For it was then, in a sudden flash of icy cold clarity, that Bill realized the awful truth. They hadn't made it across the bridge after all. They had been killed, just as this newspaper was reporting. And now, like the original Flying Dutchman ship that forever sailed the seas, he and his family were doomed to travel these roads in search of a destination they would never reach.

Drifting slowly back to the car like the ghost he now realized he was, Bill found his mother and father waiting for him impatiently.

"I think I know how to get to the interstate now," his father announced proudly. "Hop in. We should be there in less than an hour."

Letting the newspaper drop to the street, Bill silently slid into the car's backseat and firmly shut the door. As they pulled away from New Amsterdam, he looked back and watched as its distinctive windmill grew smaller and smaller, then finally disappeared from sight. Somehow he knew they'd be back sooner rather than later. And they would return again and again until the universe itself came to an end.

into thin air

As he prepared to address the student assembly, the police detective stepped to the podium wearing a serious expression. "As you may have heard, there have been a number of disappearances over the past week," he began. "We need all of you kids to be extra careful. This means walking in groups whenever possible, not going out after dark without an adult, and reporting any suspicious characters you see hanging around the school or in the nearby parks."

Leslie Green tried not to fidget in her chair, but the police officer's speech was giving her the creeps. She knew all too well that the area around Riverside Junior High had been the site of at least four disappearances since the previous Wednesday, and she knew that all of the missing people were students.

The first kid to vanish was a seventh grader named Scott Bradshaw. According to the news reports, Scott disappeared while riding his bicycle home through White Water Park. No trace of either the boy or his bike was found. Leslie remembered Scott as being a small, nerdy kid who nobody would have noticed was missing if his dad wasn't the owner of the largest factory in town.

The next kid to go was Susan Dannen, a tall, pretty girl who everyone had figured would someday grow up to be a big-time movie star. The story was that Susan had gone out to the local convenience store to buy a copy of *Modern Hollywood* magazine and never returned. Both of the clerks at the store were questioned thoroughly, but neither of them remembered Susan even coming in that day. Like Scott, Susan had simply vanished into thin air.

At first kidnapping was suspected, but when no ransom notes appeared, new theories were proposed, ranging from alien abduction to murder. Soon word spread that a serial killer was loose—this despite the fact that no bodies were found, and there was no other physical evidence of foul play. Still, parents were afraid and kept their children close to home. That, however, didn't prevent Wesley Robbins, a chunky eighth grader who played goalie for the school soccer team, and Rebecca Thomas, the best cellist in the school orchestra, from disappearing on their way to school.

Now every kid at Riverside Junior High was fearing for his or her life. Passing one another in the halls, they eyed each other as if wondering who the next victim was going to be. And, consequently, they all hung on every word the police detective was saying.

"Remember, we need each and every one of you to be on your toes and to act with common sense," the detective warned. "And if any of you have information about these disappearances, it's important that you come forward. If you don't want to give your name, you can always call the police hotline anonymously at 1-800-HELPOUT."

A second policeman came forward and gave the four hundred students in the auditorium a crash course in self-defense. But while everyone else paid close attention, Leslie hardly listened at all. She figured that if the kidnapper ever tried to nab her, the best thing she could do was scream and run.

Recognizing the kidnapper would be easy. She'd seen enough true-to-life TV shows to put together a pretty good profile of such a person. It would probably be a man between thirty-five and forty-five years old with some kind of an evil look about him, like a stubbly-bearded face, shifty-looking eyes, and a constant snarl on his lips.

Yes, Leslie Green figured she knew exactly what to look out for. Unfortunately she couldn't have been more wrong.

■ ■ ■ ■

That same afternoon Leslie grabbed her backpack and started straight for home. Since the disappearances her mom and dad—just like all the other parents in the area—wanted their kids to come straight home from school, with no stops at the convenience store, the frozen yogurt shop, the video arcade, or even a friend's house. In fact, some parents were so concerned that they showed up at school to actually *drive* their children home, even if they lived as close as a block away. Fortunately Leslie's mom and dad hadn't gotten that paranoid, but they did demand that she get home after school without delay.

Leslie followed the usual route that would take her down Rayburn Street, then through a narrow alley between the Griffith Hardware Store and Manfred's Hobby Shop to Pierce

Avenue. From there it was just another half-block up Mulberry Road to her house.

The walk down Rayburn Street passed without incident. It was the middle of the afternoon and the sidewalks were crowded with shoppers as well as students on their way home from school. But when she reached the alley between the Griffith Hardware Store and Manfred's Hobby Shop, Leslie's pace slowed as a cold chill ran down her spine. Today the brick-lined passageway seemed even narrower than usual, and although it hadn't rained in at least a week, the alley had a damp, musty odor that Leslie never noticed before.

For the first time in her life—after walking down this alley countless times before—Leslie was scared to the bone. With so many kids disappearing, walking through such a dark, creepy passageway was like begging for disaster.

At the same time going all the way around the block seemed like an enormous waste of effort. She could walk down this alley and be out the other side in a mere thirty seconds. Taking the long route would require at least a full five minutes. Plus, she figured the odds of some crazed killer just happening to be lurking in this alley at the very moment she decided to walk through it were pretty slim.

"Be brave, Leslie," she muttered under her breath as she strode purposefully into the dark alley. "You have nothing to fear but fear itself."

Maybe it was just her imagination, but almost as soon as she entered the narrow passageway, all the sounds from the outside world seemed to drop away. The rumble of the cars on Rayburn Street, the scraping of shoppers' shoes on the sidewalk, the squeaking of bicycle brakes—they all seemed to fade away to practically nothing. In their place, Leslie heard only the rapid beating of her own heart and the hoarse passage of air in and out of her lungs as she moved as rapidly as she could toward the safety of the light at the alley's opposite end.

But as strange as it seemed, the faster Leslie walked, the farther the exit seemed to become. It was as if the alley had become rubberized, and some great unseen force was stretching it ahead of her, forcing her to work harder and harder to make less and less progress.

On the verge of panic, she was only halfway through the alley when someone appeared in the opening ahead, blocking the light. Instantly Leslie stopped in her tracks and prepared to scream.

It's the kidnapper! she thought. He's come to get me!

But as the stranger stumbled toward her, Leslie saw that this was not an adult but someone about her own age. And it wasn't a man at all—it was a girl, dressed in badly torn clothes.

"Help me," the girl groaned.

Slowly Leslie recognized who was under the grime-coated face. It was someone she'd seen many times before.

"Susan Dannen!" Leslie cried, recognizing the girl as the second person to have vanished in the last week.

Susan stumbled forward and urgently grabbed Leslie's arm. "You have to help me," she gasped.

"What happened?" Leslie asked nervously. "Where have you been? Are you all right?"

"Come with me!" Susan demanded. "We've got to help the other kids!"

"You mean the others are still alive?" Leslie cried.

"For now," Susan replied gravely. "But not for long unless we save them."

"Wait!" Leslie insisted, struggling to remain calm. "We can't do this alone. We've got to call the police."

"No time," Susan gasped. "We have to go now!"

She continued to tug on Leslie's arm, dragging her toward the alley's far end.

"All right," Leslie agreed reluctantly. "But where are we going? Where are the others?"

"Follow me," was all Susan said.

Seconds later Leslie and Susan were out of the alley and heading down Pierce Avenue. The street traffic here was much lighter than it was on Rayburn, so there was no one Leslie could call to for help even if Susan had let her.

From Pierce Avenue they ran through White Water Park, the site of Scott Bradshaw's disappearance. Finally they made their way past old warehouses to a lot where several old railroad tanker cars—the kind used to transport heating oil and toxic chemicals—had stood rusting since this section of train track had been abandoned years before.

"They're in there," Susan said breathlessly, pointing to one of the cylindrical-shaped railroad cars. She started for the ladder that led to the tanker's entrance hatch, but Leslie pulled her back.

"Wait a minute," Leslie said, not wanting to get herself trapped like the others. "First I want some answers. Who's been kidnapping these kids, and why? And how did you get away?"

Susan looked around nervously. "There's just no time to explain," she insisted. "When the others are safe, I can tell you the whole story. Let's go before he gets *you*, too!"

With that Susan pulled herself free and started up the old, rusty ladder. Leslie wanted to run, to get as far away from this place as she could and call the police. But if Susan was right, at least three more lives were depending on her.

Mustering her courage, she grabbed hold of the ladder on the side of the tanker car and struggled to pull herself up. Susan was waiting for her by the entrance hatch.

"Help me with this," Susan said, putting her hand on the wheel that opened the hatch. Leslie grabbed the other side, and together they turned the stiff wheel until the lock slid free. Then, still working together, they lifted the heavy metal hatch and peered down into the dark, empty tank below.

"Hello!" Leslie called. "Is anybody in there?"

"Yes!" a boy's voice called back. "It's me! Scott Bradshaw!"

"And Wesley Robbins!" another boy shouted.

"And Rebecca Thomas!" a girl chimed in. "Who are you?"

"Leslie Green!" Leslie shouted down. "I'm here with Susan Dannen! We're going to get you out!"

"No!" Wesley called up. "Don't come down here! Don't let her—"

But it was too late. As Leslie was leaning down into the hatchway, Susan gave her a powerful shove from behind, which caused Leslie to plunge headfirst into the tanker car.

Her arms stretched out before her, Leslie slammed into an old mattress. Stunned and confused, she came to her senses in the dark, and she looked back up through the hatchway into Susan's grinning face.

"Sorry about that, old pal," Susan said with a laugh. "You gotta watch that first step. It's a doozy."

Leslie looked at the three other captives. Each looked tired and worn out, but otherwise seemed unharmed. As her eyes adjusted to the gloom, she could see that the interior of the tanker car had been filled with boxes of junk food, cans of soda, comic books, and all the other necessities of junior-high-school life. In addition, each of the kids was holding a battery-powered flashlight, the kind with the magnetized handles that allowed you to attach them to metal walls, automobile hoods—or the interior walls of tanker cars.

"What's going on?" Leslie asked, confused.

"Susan's going to hold us for ransom," Scott explained. "Now that she has all four of us, she's going to demand ten thousand dollars apiece for our return."

"Including ten thousand dollars from her own parents who think she's been kidnapped, too!" Rebecca added.

"But why?" Leslie demanded, looking up at Susan's still-smiling face ten feet above. "Why do you need that money?"

"Why, to be a movie star, of course," Susan replied matter-of-factly from the top of the tanker car. "With fifty thousand bucks I can buy myself a plane ticket to Hollywood, take acting lessons, have my photos taken, and buy myself a glamorous wardrobe. With all that I can get an agent who'll get me into the movies." She paused and flashed everyone her biggest, brightest movie-star smile. "Oh, I know I'll have to begin with small parts, of course. But with my beauty and talent, it won't be long before I start getting starring roles. Maybe I'll even have my own TV show one day. I figure it will take at least a year, and in the meantime, I'll still have money to live on. Pretty clever plan, wouldn't you say?"

Leslie glanced into the faces of her fellow captives. They all wore the same terrified, exhausted expression. They knew Susan meant business.

"She's crazy," Scott whispered.

Leslie rolled her eyes. "No kidding."

"Well, I've got to go," Susan said, preparing to shut the hatch on them.

"Wait!" Leslie shouted back.

Susan hesitated. "What is it?" she asked. "I'm in a hurry."

"You forgot just one thing," Leslie declared. "When you let us go, we'll be able to identify you, and you won't get very far in your career with half the cops in the country looking for you."

"What do you think I am, dumb or something?" Susan replied snidely. "I'm going to have plastic surgery. I'll change my face, my hair color, maybe even the way I walk. And, of course, I'll change my name. All the movie stars in Hollywood do that anyway!"

Leslie suddenly found herself at a loss for words. It seemed that Susan had, indeed, figured this plan out down to the last detail. It could be just crazy enough to work.

"Now, if you'll excuse me, I've got some ransom notes to write," Susan said. "See you at the movies!"

And with that Susan started to close the heavy metal hatch. Leslie knew she had to do something fast, or she'd be trapped in here along with the other hostages . . . for who knows how long?

"Give me that!" she shouted to Rebecca, and immediately snatched the flashlight out of the startled girl's hand. In the same move, Leslie tossed the flashlight straight up into the air. With a metallic *clang*! its magnetic handle attached itself to the inner edge of the hatch's underside. Susan started to slam the hatch shut, but with the flashlight now wedged beneath the hinge, there was no way she could fully close it.

"Quick—boost me up!" Leslie ordered to the others as Susan tried to figure out what was jamming the hatch.

Working together, Scott, Wesley, and Rebecca lifted Leslie up toward the hatchway. Then while Susan was still trying to force the hatch to close, Leslie balanced herself on the others' shoulders, set her shoulder against the hatch, and pushed with all her might.

The hatch popped open, and Leslie could hear Susan scream as the motion made the deranged girl lose her balance and slip off the top of the tanker car. Grabbing the hatchway's rim, Leslie strained with every muscle in her being as she pulled herself out of the tanker and back into the bright light of day.

Getting her bearings, Leslie saw Susan on the ground ten feet below, still dazed from her unexpected fall. Immediately Leslie scrambled down the ladder and managed to grab the would-be movie star just as she dizzily stumbled to her feet.

"Sorry, Susan," Leslie said with a smile. "But the only TV show you're going to be on is the six o'clock news."

■ ■ ■ ■

The entire town breathed a collective sigh of relief when people heard that the mysterious kidnapper had been captured and that the hostages were safe. Naturally there was a lot of talk when it was revealed that the disappearances were the result of a thirteen-year-old girl's crazed desire to be rich and famous. Some people thought Susan should be sent to a reform school. Others thought she needed a good psychiatrist. And still others—mostly newspeople from out of town—wanted the exclusive to her story.

Within days, just about every newspaper and magazine in the Western world had run at least one story about Susan Dannen. TV and movie producers clamored for her story. Publishers offered her thousands of dollars to write a book about her experience. Ironically, just for wanting to be a movie star, Susan had become more famous than most real actresses ever get.

As for Leslie Green, she was happy just to be safe and sound back in her own home. Although her telephone rang day and night, and reporters never stopped coming to her door for interviews, all she wanted was to be left alone. Despite what everyone said, she didn't consider herself a hero. She was just someone who'd been in the wrong place at the wrong time and was lucky enough to get out in one piece.

Finally Susan was packed off to a psychiatric hospital and things around Riverside Junior High began to return to normal. Kids came and went without the fear of disappearing, and they were allowed to hang out at the convenience store, the yogurt shop, and the video arcade just like before.

Leslie finally got enough courage to start walking home again through the alley between the Griffith Hardware Store and Manfred's Hobby Shop. No longer did the short walk between the buildings seem endlessly long or nearly as threatening.

But then one day after school, as Leslie was just about to emerge from the alley, she was grabbed from behind. A hand was clamped over her mouth, preventing her from screaming. Then Leslie heard a voice that was all too familiar.

"I escaped from the mental hospital," Susan Dannen said through clenched teeth. "I noticed that the papers have already stopped running anything about me. My popularity is going down, and that can only mean one thing, Leslie. Yes, old pal, it's time for a sequel!"

joy ride revisited

Laura Chapman had not planned on staying at the Creekside Shopping Mall so late. The original idea was to hang out, people watch, and maybe grab a frozen yogurt with her friends Gina Watson and Alicia Angorn until the mall's shops closed at 9:00 P.M. Then they'd take the Grant Avenue bus back to their neighborhood and be home well ahead of their 9:30 Friday night curfew. It was a simple plan, and Laura hadn't anticipated any problems. After all, she'd done this dozens of times before with no hassles whatsoever.

But on this Friday night something totally unexpected happened—Laura Chapman met a boy.

And not just any boy.

He was a head taller than Laura, had muscles like a star athlete, and the face of a movie hunk. When his dark eyes looked into Laura's big brown ones, it was as if an electric current shot right through her body. She'd never felt anything like it before in her life.

His name was Paul Barnes, and Laura first noticed him while she was browsing through the NEW RELEASES section at the music store. He was flipping through the OLDIES when all of a sudden he looked up, locked his eyes with hers, and smiled. Laura was so overwhelmed her face flushed red and she had to turn away in embarrassment.

"That guy's looking at me!" she whispered to Gina, who was next to her flipping through the CDs trying to find a birthday present for her cousin.

"Who?" Gina asked, looking blindly about.

"That cute guy over in the OLDIES," Laura said, struggling to keep from looking his way. "The tall one with the dark, wavy hair."

"I don't see anyone," Gina said with a shrug.

Concerned, Laura looked back to where she'd seen the boy . . . but he was gone.

"He was there a second ago," she insisted. "And he was smiling right at me."

"Who?" Alicia asked, walking up.

"Oh, Laura's in love with some guy who just vanished into thin air," Gina said with a sarcastic laugh.

Alicia rolled her eyes. "Come on," she said, linking her arms through those of her friends. "Let's check out Shoes Unlimited."

Laura all but forgot about the mysterious stranger until she saw him again, this time standing outside an electronics store. She and her friends were on the escalator heading up to the mall's second level when she noticed him on the floor below. As before, while she was staring at him, he turned her way, made eye contact, then smiled.

"Gina, that's him!" Laura whispered, pointing down to the first level. "That's the guy I saw at the music store!"

"Where?" Gina and Alicia asked in unison, turning in the direction where Laura was pointing. But no sooner had they turned than the escalator carried them out of view, and the mystery boy vanished from sight.

"This way!" Laura shouted as she ran down the walkway, trying to get a better view. Alicia and Gina caught up with her a few seconds later.

"Well?" Alicia asked impatiently. "Where *is* this guy?"

"He must have gone inside," Laura replied, disappointed. "But you should have seen him. He was the hottest hunk I've ever seen!" She paused a moment, then blurted out, "I'm going to try to find him!"

"What?" Gina cried in disbelief. "And what exactly do you plan to say to him if you *do* find him?"

"I don't know," Laura said. "It's just that, when he smiled at me, I felt some kind of, well, connection."

"You're crazy, Laura," Alicia said disapprovingly. "He's probably just a big flirt."

"Alicia's right," Gina agreed. "You're just asking for trouble. Besides, if it's meant to be, you'll probably run into him again."

Laura thought about what Gina had just said. "Maybe you're right," she said. "But then again, it doesn't hurt to help fate along a little, does it?" Her eyes brightened. "Look, you two, go do what you want," Laura said, waving her friends off. "But I'm going to find him. I'll meet you at the bus stop at ten minutes after nine, OK?"

Not waiting for her friends to argue with her, Laura turned and ran for the down escalator. Watching her go, Alicia and Gina shook their heads in disbelief.

"Hopeless," Alicia said with a sigh.

"Sometimes I wonder where that girl's priorities are," Gina agreed. Then she looked at her watch. "Come on, let's check out Fashion Explosion."

■ ■ ■ ■

As Laura walked through the mall searching for the mystery boy, she felt a sour feeling in the pit of her stomach. What am I doing? she wondered. Am I crazy, chasing after a total stranger? I don't know anything about him. For all I know, he could be a serial killer!

Cautiously Laura peered through the large window of the electronics store where she'd last seen the boy. There were a half-dozen shoppers browsing through the shelves, but none of them looked like the cute guy who'd smiled at her.

Laura was just about to turn away when she felt a tap on her right shoulder. Startled, she spun around and nearly screamed when she saw the boy she'd been pursuing standing directly in front of her. But her fears instantly melted away when he flashed his adorable smile and locked his dark, brooding eyes with hers.

"Hi," he said awkwardly. "I didn't mean to scare you."

"M-me? Scared? N-no problem," Laura stammered, prying her eyes away from his.

"I saw you over at the music store a while ago, and you looked familiar," the boy went on. "Didn't you used to go to Hampton Grammar School?"

"That's right," Laura said, already starting to feel more comfortable with him. "Did you?"

"A long time ago," the boy said. "I was a few grades ahead of you. My name's Paul Barnes."

With a confident smile, he offered his hand. Laura only hesitated a moment before shaking it.

"I'm Laura Chapman," she said. "I'm at Belmont Junior High now. I'll be going to Hoover High next year."

"Great school. You'll like it," Paul said. But before Laura could ask him what grade he was in, Paul pointed toward the food court. "Would you like to get some frozen yogurt?"

Laura had just had some frozen yogurt with her friends, but she wasn't about to decline Paul's invitation now. "Sure," she said with a smile. "Their chocolate-banana combo with peanut sprinkles is excellent."

For the next hour Paul and Laura ate yogurt, talked, shopped, talked, played pinball, and talked. At a store called Jericho Gifts, Laura fell madly in love with a ceramic cat that was on sale for just five dollars. Seeing how much she wanted it, Paul not only bought it for her, but paid an extra dollar for a fancy gift bag.

Although Paul was sixteen and she was two years younger, Laura found they had a lot in common. They both loved long walks, pizza with pineapple on it, TV talk shows, and oldies music from the 1980s. In fact, when their conversation turned to music, Paul couldn't even name a single contemporary band he liked. For him, music had hit its zenith a full decade earlier.

"The eighties were great," Paul said as they strolled past a row of fashion stores. "I mean, they had great music, great movies, and great cars. It was a fantastic time to be alive."

"I guess," Laura replied awkwardly. "I was only an infant at the time. You're so much older than I am."

"Not really," Paul said. "I guess it all depends on when your memory kicks in, whether a thing means something personal to you or it doesn't."

119

Wow, Laura thought as she fell into Paul's mesmerizing eyes. This guy is really deep!

It was then that she noticed that all the stores they were passing had closed up for the night, and the mall itself was practically deserted. Concerned, she glanced at her watch and saw that the time was already 9:05.

"It's so late!" Laura cried. "I'm supposed to meet my friends at the bus stop in five minutes!"

Clutching the bag containing her new ceramic cat, Laura turned and ran toward the escalators. When she glanced back, she saw that Paul was still standing where she'd left him.

"Come on!" she called back, waving for him to follow. "I want you to meet my friends!"

"You go on ahead!" he shouted back. "I'll get my car and meet you at the bus stop!"

Laura didn't want to leave Paul behind, but knew she had no choice. If she missed her bus and didn't get home before 9:30, her folks would be so mad she'd be grounded for a month.

Her heart racing, Laura bounded up the moving escalator steps, bolted down a side hallway, and burst out the mall's main entrance just in time to see the Grant Avenue bus leaving.

"No!" she shouted, waving her arms madly for the bus to stop. "Come back!" But it was too late.

Depressed, Laura was standing at the vacant bus stop, and imagining the long, lonely mile-long walk back to her house when she heard a car horn. She turned just as Paul, sitting at the wheel of a gleaming red 1985 Mustang convertible, pulled up. Although over a decade old, the car looked good as new.

"Need a lift?" he asked with a smile.

"I sure do," Laura said, sighing with relief. "I live about eight blocks from here, just off Grant Avenue. That's not going to be out of your way, is it?"

"Not at all," Paul said, leaning over to open the passenger door for her. "In fact, I was going in that direction anyway. Hop in."

Laura was about to climb into the car when she hesitated again. She remembered her parents' warnings about getting into cars with strangers. Even now that she was almost in high school, they regularly warned her about the dangers of hitch-hiking and told her stories about what often happened to young girls who rode off with people they didn't know. These stories never had happy endings.

"Well?" Paul asked. "What are you waiting for?"

Laura looked Paul over, then took another look at his car. Although she'd only known the boy for an hour, they'd spent so much time talking that she felt like they'd been friends for weeks. She had good feelings about Paul Barnes, and when it came to judging a person's character, she was usually right.

"Thanks," Laura said with a smile as she slid in next to Paul, then shut her door.

"Buckle up," Paul reminded her, reaching over to help her with the seat belt.

Laura liked that Paul was concerned for her safety. And she also liked the way it felt when his arm brushed against hers.

I hope we can be friends, she thought. And in another year or so . . . who knows? Maybe there can be something special between us.

When Laura was secured, Paul gripped the steering wheel, then gently pressed the accelerator. The car eased forward into the parking lot, toward the exit.

"You've got a great car," Laura remarked, running her hand along the dashboard.

"Like it?" Paul asked, flashing a killer grin. "I just got it yesterday for my sixteenth birthday. She's a beaut, isn't she?"

"What year is it?" asked Laura.

"Eighty-five," Paul replied.

Laura glanced at the instrument panel and noticed that the car's odometer showed only one hundred miles on it!

"One hundred miles in ten years?" Laura looked amazed. "Was this car sitting in someone's garage all this time?"

"Hang on," Paul said, ignoring her. "Let me show you what this baby can do." He slammed his foot on the accelerator and the Mustang lurched forward.

Frightened, Laura felt herself being pressed back in her seat as the car shot down Grant Avenue like a rocket.

"Ya-hooooooo!" Paul yelled crazily as they shot through an intersection . . . *and* a red light. He turned to Laura, his hair blowing in the wind. "Isn't this a blast?" he shouted.

Laura saw that the speedometer was now hovering just under sixty miles per hour—in a forty mile-per-hour zone! She wondered how long it would be before Paul wrapped them around a light pole or a cop pulled them over.

"Slow down!" Laura pleaded. "You're going too fast!"

"Naw, this isn't fast!" Paul said with a leer. "This is fast!"

He shifted gears, and the convertible abruptly accelerated up to seventy miles per hour. Unable to hold back any longer, Laura screamed. Paul, who seemed so kind and sweet back at the mall, had suddenly become a raving madman!

"Stop the car!" she ordered.

"What?!" Paul cried over the roar of the engine.

"I said, *stop the car!*" Laura screamed, pulling on his arm.

"I can't hear you!" Paul shouted back, obviously toying with her. "What did you say?"

Gritting her teeth, Laura grabbed the gearshift, preparing to yank it into neutral, when Paul saw her and nearly went berserk.

"Don't touch that!" he shouted. "You'll hurt the car!"

He released the accelerator and slammed on the brakes. With an ear-piercing screech, the Mustang skidded to a stop just a half block from Laura's house. Without missing a beat, Laura unbuckled her seat belt, threw open her door, and scrambled out of the car.

"Thanks for the ride," she gasped. "I'll walk from here."

"You sure you don't want to drive around some more?" Paul asked calmly as if what he'd just done was the most natural thing in the world.

"I'm very sure," Laura said, staggering backward, her legs feeling like rubber.

"What's your phone number?" Paul inquired. "Maybe we can go out sometime."

"Actually, my parents don't let me go out with sixteen-year-olds," Laura lied as she continued to back away. "But maybe I'll see you around the mall again sometime."

"If that's the way you want it, fine," Paul said, suddenly cold and distant. "See you around."

With that he threw his car into gear and, burning rubber, shot back onto Grant Avenue. Laura watched the Mustang fly like a missile on wheels until it vanished into the dark night. Then, sighing with relief that she was still in one piece, she staggered off toward home.

It wasn't until she reached her front door that it occurred to Laura that she'd left the bag with her ceramic cat in Paul's front seat. She figured it was a small price to pay for getting out of the car alive.

■ ■ ■ ■

The next morning Gina and Alicia were all over Laura with a barrage of questions from the moment she arrived at school.

"What happened to you last night?" Gina demanded. "How come you didn't catch the bus?"

"Did you finally meet your dream guy?" Alicia asked in a teasing way.

"He was more like a *nightmare* guy," Laura replied. She went on to tell her friends the whole awful adventure. When she got to the end of her tale, she noticed that Gina and Alicia were looking at her oddly.

"What's wrong?" Laura asked.

"What did you say this guy's name was?" Alicia asked.

"Paul Barnes," Laura responded. "Why?"

Alicia and Gina shared another nervous glance before they turned back to their friend.

"My older brother, Max, knew a guy named Paul Barnes," Gina revealed.

"Maybe this is the same guy," Laura suggested.

"I said, he *knew* Paul Barnes," Gina emphasized. "Paul Barnes died over ten years ago . . . when he was sixteen. He'd just gotten a new Mustang as a birthday present, and was killed speeding down Grant Avenue."

For a long time, Laura just stood there in awed silence. Could it be that she'd spent the previous evening with a ghost—a ghost who'd almost gotten her killed, too?

"But th-that's impossible," Laura stammered, her voice cracking. "There's no way!"

Beginning to tremble from the odd chill creeping up her spine, she turned away, ran down the hall, and burst out of the school. She ran and ran until, for reasons she didn't quite understand, she found herself stopping at the entrance to the West Side Cemetery. Drawn by irresistible curiosity, she walked slowly through the wrought iron front gate and began moving down the various rows, checking the names on the headstones.

124

It took her nearly an hour to find the particular headstone she'd been looking for. There it was, carved in red granite, the name, "Paul Barnes" and the dates "1969–1985."

But it was what was resting at the foot of the headstone that really chilled Laura to the bone. It was a paper bag bearing the logo of Jericho Gifts. Her hands shaking in fear, Laura carefully opened the bag.

Inside was her ceramic cat.

As she stood there, clutching the tiny statue to her chest, a cold wind suddenly blew through the cemetery. And with it came a sound. It sounded like a distant car engine, and soon it was joined by the wild, reckless laugh of a boy on a joyride to infinity.

COLLECT ALL THE SCARES YOU'VE EVER DREAMED OF AT YOUR FAVORITE BOOKSTORE!

If you are unable to find these titles at your bookstore, fill in the Quantity Column for each title described, and order directly from Price Stern Sloan.

Mail order form to:
PUTNAM PUBLISHING GROUP
Mail Order Department
Department B
P.O. Box 12289
Newark, NJ 07101-5289

FAX (201) 933-2316
☎ (800) 788-6262
☎ (201) 933-9292
On a touch-tone phone, hit prompt 1

Collect all the terrifying titles in the Scary Stories for Sleep-Overs series . . .

ISBN #	Quantity	Title	US price	Can. price
0-8431-2914-X	_____	Scary Stories for Sleep-Overs	$4.95	$6.50
0-8431-3451-8	_____	More Scary Stories for Sleep-Overs	$4.95	$6.50
0-8431-3588-3	_____	Still More Scary Stories for Sleep-Overs	$4.95	$6.50
0-8431-3746-0	_____	Even More Scary Stories for Sleep-Overs	$4.95	$6.50
0-8431-3915-3	_____	Super Scary Stories for Sleep-Overs	$4.95	$6.75
0-8431-3916-1	_____	More Super Scary Stories for Sleep-Overs	$4.95	$6.75
0-8431-8219-9	_____	Mega Scary Stories for Sleep-Overs	$5.95	$7.95

And check out the titles in this brand new scary *and* spine-tingling series . . .

ISBN #	Quantity	Title	US price	Can. price
0-8431-8220-2	_____	Scary Mysteries for Sleep-Overs	$5.95	$7.95
0-8431-8221-0	_____	More Scary Mysteries for Sleep-Overs	$5.95	$7.95

Now dive into NIGHTMARES! HOW WILL YOURS END? — Each title has over 20 endings!

ISBN #	Quantity	Title	US price	Can. price
0-8431-3862-9	_____	Castle of Horror	$4.50	$5.95
0-8431-3861-0	_____	Cave of Fear	$4.50	$5.95
0-8431-3860-2	_____	Planet of Terror	$4.50	$5.95
0-8431-3863-7	_____	Valley of the Screaming Statues	$4.50	$5.95

All orders must be prepaid in US funds

❑ Check or Money Order
❑ Visa
❑ Mastercard-Interbank
❑ American Express
❑ International Money Order or Bank Draft

Expiration Date _____

Signature _____

Daytime phone # _____

Postage/Handling Charges as Follows:

$2.50 for first book
$0.75 each additional book
(Maximum shipping charge of $6.25)

Merchandise total	$_____
Shipping/Handling	$_____
Applicable Sales Tax (CA, NJ, NY, VA)	$_____
GST (Canada)	$_____
Total Amount (US currency only)	$_____

Minimum order $15.00

NOTE: Prices and handling charges are subject to change without notice, but we will always ship the least expensive edition available. Please allow 4 to 6 weeks for delivery.

Refer to source: SCARY